BREATH OF DEATH . . .

A chill, moist wind off the sea brushed over Dr. Raymond Barr and three members of the Scum of the Earth as they crouched on the rooftop of the Hotel San Juan. Occasional spatters of rain fell from the clouds that obscured the sky, threatening a real downpour. Even without the overhead murk, this was an ideal night, in the dark of the moon. They huddled near the wheezing, old-fashioned air-conditioning system, working as quietly as possible.

"We're ready, Doc," Brad Lessor whispered.

"Fine," Dr. Barr replied, releasing the valve on his aerosol cylinder. "Here it comes." His mind filled in the hissing he could not actually hear as the deadly Beta Globulin X spewed out into the ventilating system. A beatific smile spread over his face.

Below the hovering forms on the roof, in the banquet room, over a hundred of the nation's most notable black citizens were gathered. Among the conventioneers sat doctors, lawyers, clergymen, and entertainers. Half a dozen well-known sports figures graced the head table. As guests, they were being feted to the best the island could provide. They were looking forward to the address by Dr. Alfonso de Vega, outspoken head of the Puerto Rican independence movement.

Everyone present was unaware that Death had become the master of ceremonies. . . .

THE PENETRATOR SERIES:

#1 THE TARGET IS H
#2 BLOOD ON THE STRIP
#3 CAPITOL HELL
#4 HIJACKING MANHATTAN
#5 MARDI GRAS MASSACRE
#6 TOKYO PURPLE
#7 BAJA BANDIDOS
#8 THE NORTHWEST CONTRACT
#9 DODGE CITY BOMBERS
#10 THE HELLBOMB FLIGHT
#11 TERROR IN TAOS
#12 BLOODY BOSTON
#13 DIXIE DEATH SQUAD
#14 MANKILL SPORT
#15 THE QUEBEC CONNECTION
#16 DEEPSEA SHOOTOUT
#17 DEMENTED EMPIRE
#18 COUNTDOWN TO TERROR
#19 PANAMA POWER PLAY
#20 THE RADIATION HIT
#21 THE SUPERGUN MISSION
#22 HIGH DISASTER
#23 DIVINE DEATH
#24 CRYOGENIC NIGHTMARE
#25 FLOATING DEATH
#26 MEXICAN DEATH
#27 THE ANIMAL GAME
#28 THE SKYHIGH BETRAYERS
#29 ARYAN ONSLAUGHT
#30 COMPUTER KILL
#31 OKLAHOMA FIREFIGHT
#32 SHOWBIZ WIPEOUT
#33 SATELLITE SLAUGHTER
#34 DEATH RAY TERROR
#35 BLACK MASSACRE

NO. 35

THE PENETRATOR

BLACK MASSACRE

by Lionel Derrick

PINNACLE BOOKS LOS ANGELES

PENETRATOR #35: BLACK MASSACRE

An original Pinnacle Books edition, published for the first time anywhere.

First printing, March 1980

ISBN: 0-523-40632-0

Special acknowledgments to Mark Roberts

Cover illustration by George Wilson

Photos for illustrations in Combat Catalog courtesy Toro Photography and Ahl Foto

Printed in the United States of America

PINNACLE BOOKS, INC.
2029 Century Park East
Los Angeles, California 90067

This one's for Andy, Joe and Art . . . with fond memories of Mercing with *Los Gatos de Oro*.

L.D.

CONTENTS

BLACK MASSACRE

PROLOGUE

He left a name, at which the world grew pale,
To point a moral, or adorn a tale.
—Johnson, on the
Power of a Name.

"Hey, Lucas," Brad Overlin, city editor for the *Denver Post* called to his top reporter. "You remember back awhile when that guy was raisin' hell around here, you know, the Penetrator?"

Terry Lucas brightened, sitting upright in his ancient, armless, wooden swivel chair. "Yeah. What about it?"

"You did some fine articles on it. Seems like you got close to him, right?"

Lucas hesitated. "Yeah . . . you might say that."

"Might, hell, man. You held down this end of his campaign against those freako cultists. At least that's what the police seem to think. Wow! We coulda had a Jonestown right here if it hadn't been for that guy."

"So what's this got to do with here and now? You want me to run a comparison between the People's Temple and the Church of the Final Coming? It's a little late for that now."

"Naw. Listen, Terry, would you believe that the Penetrator has fan clubs?"

Terry Lucas blinked. "You're kidding."

"Gospel. They're supposed to be all over the country. Some guy on the AP wire put it through last night when there was nothin' else of interest. 'Penetratoring' they call it. Sort of a takeoff on 'Trekking' and the Trekees who are freaked out over 'Star Trek.' I did some checking this morning with the PD intelligence unit. By God, we got a chapter here in Denver."

"I'll be damned." To cover his suddenly excited interest, Terry Lucas rearranged his features and spoke with bored cynicism. "And?"

"I want you to look into them. See what makes them tick. Might be worth a column and a half on the city page."

"On what? A clutch of daydreaming high schoolers with acne and some militant little old ladies in tennis shoes? Where do I start with something like that?"

"You start with Mr. Arthur Bowman."

Mr. Arthur Bowman had neither acne nor tennis shoes. He sat behind the large, cluttered desk in the manager's office of International Home Credit, looking natty and competent in a subdued blue-gray broadcloth suit, with matching vest, cream-tone shirt, and follard tie. His dark, curly hair and engaging grin removed Terry Lucas's worst doubts about a Penetrator "fan."

"So you want to know about Penetratoring, Mr. Lucas?" Bowman flashed his warm smile again. "If you're the Terry Lucas I think you are, I should be interviewing you . . . or asking you to speak at our next meeting."

Terry flushed. "I see my fame . . . or infamy . . . has preceded me."

"Infamy! Far from it." Bowman's voice changed, a winsome, awe-filled tone entering it. "Oh, to have been a part of just one of his missions. Fantastic."

"All I did was answer a few telephone calls, keep the cops off his back. Hell, the locals and feds grilled me for two days after it was over."

"And you didn't tell them a thing. You know, you're one of us at heart."

"How did this . . . Penetratoring get started?" Terry asked, seeking to get back to the reason for his being there.

"I'm not all that sure how it got going nationally. For my own part, I didn't even believe there was such a person as the Penetrator until after that thing in New York. Remember that? The black militants trying to hold the entire city for ransom? Adding all that to what happened in L.A., that heroin operation he busted up, then Vegas and Washington, D.C. Well, I became a believer. Then there came New Orleans, Tokyo, Baja California, Seattle, Dodge City," Bowman said, reciting a well-known and revered litany.

"What about that nut scientist in Utah stealing satellites? Then that Indian uprising in Taos, on to Boston, Georgia, British Columbia, Quebec, and France, the Bahamas, busting that Syndicate thing in Florida, Nebraska, and Guatemala. God, the man's incredible. I'd just left New York when he came back there after that Puerto Rican gang. Then to Panama.

"Sure made the government look stupid, denying

all the time that there were Cuban troops in Panama and him getting into a firefight with them. Did you know he'd been in Colorado before taking on Levu and his kook cult? Yeah. After some paranoids, who didn't believe in nuclear power plants, decided to kill a few people to make their point. Then he surfaced in Oklahoma and Texas, went after that screwball Senator in Oregon, and then came back here to take on the People's Temple . . . but you know all about that.

"I could go on like this for an hour," Bowman said, changing the subject. "Did you know he's made thirty-four hits so far?"

"I thought the official list was smaller than that."

"Oh, the feds try to minimize the whole thing. Afraid other people might take up the same idea, know what I mean? Like he's always going after the ones who can pay off the judges and prosecutors, or are too important and influential to be gotten to in the usual way. Besides, it makes *their* record look bad. So, whenever they haven't any definite proof, they deny the guy had anything to do with it. Take a for-instance.

"The police deny that the Penetrator had anything to do with breaking up that frozen whoresickle thing down in the islands, or had a hand in smashing that domestic oil conspiracy. And nobody is talking about that Third World satellite that suddenly stopped screwing up our weather. But those of us who are into Penetratoring can see signs of his fine hand working in there somewhere. Can you imagine it? Thirty-four missions . . . and the law is no closer to finding him than they were the day he started against Scarelli and the Mafia. I wonder where he is right now . . . what he's planning?"

"Yeah. I'd give a lot of money to know," Lucas agreed.

Mark Hardin, the man the press and everyone else called the Penetrator, lay on the white sand beach of the Gulf Coast, a quarter-mile down from the public fishing pier at Gulfport, Mississippi. The rhythmic rumble of incoming waves and the gentle sibilance of their retreat had lulled him into a semi-wakeful state. A benign smile curved the corners of his mouth and he tingled with the vibrant warmth of the sun that toasted his hard-muscled, six-foot-two body a coppery brown. Beside him on the blanket lay Angie Dillon.

Lovely, blonde Angie Dillon of Summit County, Utah, whom the Penetrator had twice sworn to himself never to see again. Every time he broke his oath, Mark cursed himself for being weak-willed, but he seemed compelled to indulge his whim, at least in this one area. Mark opened his eyes and glanced at Angie, whose body glistened with tanning lotion, her silky flesh nearly as dark as the half-Cheyenne she lay beside. Mark raised on one elbow, his attention distracted by the shrill sound of excited voices coming from the water some seventy-five yards away.

In the four-foot depths, where the breakers curled over their foam-tipped tops to crash into the beach, Angie's twins, Kevin and Karen, frolicked as near-naked as the law would allow. With youthful abandon they called to each other, brother daring sister to go out farther, to catch a bigger wave. With the agility of young porpoises, they leaped ahead of the next roller, riding it out until their bellies scraped sand, rising laughing to start out again. Watching them, Mark realized that they fully intended to enjoy each second of their unexpected, but welcome, vacation, occasioned by their eleventh birthday.

But, as always for the Penetrator, this was a working vacation. No matter how hard and carefully

Mark planned for a period of relaxation, escape from the pressures and demands of his chosen pursuits, it seemed that trouble always followed him, or lay in wait for him when he arrived at his intended retreat. This time, rumors of external pressure and internal strife, affecting a large segment of the local population, had brought him to the Gulf Coast to get a first-hand view of a situation that might or might not prove critical. Someone, it seemed, wanted to take over the shrimping industry. Not only the processors, and the fishermen themselves, but the shipyards and wholesalers as well were threatened. At least, that's what the computer printout at the Stronghold indicated might go down in the next few months. In the past, data accumulated in the Communications and Operations rooms of the Stronghold—Professor Willard Haskins's fantastic underground mansion in the Calico Mountains of California—had saved time and trouble. More importantly, it had saved lives. As nebulous as this shrimping scheme seemed, Mark wanted a personal contact, perhaps to find some key that might prevent the danger predicted by the electronic brain.

Since so soft a recon presented no possibility of combat, Mark had invited Angie and the twins to come along. Besides providing excellent and believable cover, they were fun to be with. They made him feel as though, even for a few short days, he were a part of normal life. Mark stirred from his thoughts as Angie spoke.

"You ought to see them in a pool. They're like a couple of fish."

"Natural athletes. Skiing, karate, swimming, horses . . . you'll have to watch it, or before long they'll have their own fan club, like those two kids in Hollywood—what's their names?—Jimmy and Kristy McNichol."

"Don't see why not. After all, *you* have a fan club."

"Wha . . . ?" Mark asked, not really following what Angie said. His attention had remained divided between their light banter and Kevin Dillon, who stood knee-deep in the surf, calling and gesturing for them to join him.

"I said, you have a fan club. And I'm a member."

"Angie, what are you talking about?"

"Let's face it," Angie replied, a frown of exasperation wrinkling her forehead. "You know that I know who you are, even if I don't know your real name. Can't help that," she added, almost as an aside, "with those arrowheads showing up in Summitville when you tore into the Aryan Brotherhood. The kids know, too. Yet, we've kept your secret. No one said anything. Even when they questioned us after . . . after what happened in Coalville, we didn't even talk to that ugly little creep the FBI sent, Goodman? Then, a short time ago, I heard about this thing called . . . Penetratoring. I looked into it and joined the club. So did the kids."

"Christ, Angie! That's like having a fan club for an undertaker. You can't be serious."

"I am . . . and there are chapters of the club all over the country. You're quite a celebrity, you know. The kids are crazy about it. They love thinking of themselves as being almost part of the Penetrator's family. The best part, as Karen puts it, is keeping the secret between just the three of us."

Mark, worried now, took Angie by the shoulders. "Do you realize the danger you could be in? Look, there might be people who want me in the worst possible way, watching this club, checking out the members. What happens if they find you there in Utah, tie it in with what happened to the Aryan Brotherhood? There'd be no way to protect you from them. You're so vulnerable, so enormously vulnerable."

"We might be better protected if we were close to you . . . all the time. You have to have a place, somewhere, where you keep your information, prepare for a mission. If I . . . *if we* were there, living as a family, wouldn't we be as safe together as you are alone?"

Mark let go of Angie, turned away. "Out of the question."

Angie moved in a flurry, spraying sand as she came in front of Mark, kneeling between his outstretched legs, cupping his face in her hands. "I love you, you big brute. You can't help but see that. And you love me. Now don't deny it, you can't hide a thing like that. It's in your every word, every gesture, your look, touch. And you love the kids, too. Your face gets soft and your eyes glow when you watch them working out in the *dojo*, or riding horseback, or swimming, of just lying around the living room doing homework. What is it that you're dreaming about when you get that wistful, proud look on your face? Is it . . . is it that for a little while you see Kevie and Karen as your own?"

"Drop it, Angie!" Mark's voice cracked with anguish and resignation. "This is one contest you can't win."

"I could win." Angie sensed she'd come painfully close to the truth. "If I had your name, knew who you really are. If you heard me, heard the kids, speak that name with the love we have for you . . . I'd win all right."

Mark's face closed into deep crevice-like lines of worry and he shook his head from side to side, as though struggling against a powerful and invisible force. His throat felt dry and he struggled to keep the words from getting past his lips.

"My name is Mark, Angie," he said softly, knowing as he spoke that he could well be losing the battle while barely into the first engagement. "Mark Hardin."

Chapter 1

AN AVERAGE MUGGING

Large wet flakes of heavy snow drifted on the slight breeze, glowing in the lights of the parking lot at Rock's T-Bone. Over a period of ten years, owner Cecil Rock had made the restaurant into Indianapolis's most popular supper club. Although it was quite late, more than a dozen cars still filled spots, the macadam showing in dark rectangles beneath them, where the gently falling flakes had as yet failed to insinuate themselves.

A couple, in their late forties, emerged from the main entrance of the supper club and headed toward an aged Mark IV Continental parked in the far corner of the lot. The woman was done up in mink, her husband in a knee-length, fur-trimmed, leather coat. Plumes of white issued from their mouths as they turned up their collars and commented on the unexpected snowfall. Stepping carefully, they increased the length of their stride, seeking the comfort of their car.

Crouching in a pool of darkness, amid the large metal garbage bins at the kitchen entrance to Rock's T-Bone, three forms in dark clothing remained invisible. Not until one smiled could their presence be detected. The eyes of the two juveniles and a boy of nineteen were fixed on the somewhat weaving course of Dr. Raymond Barr and his wife. Tensing, they readied themselves for action.

At the side of his Lincoln, Dr. Barr removed a key from his coat pocket and bent to insert it into the lock. At the precise instant the mechanism clicked open, the three muggers struck.

Strong, wiry arms encircled Dr. Barr, pinning his limbs to his sides, jerking him backward, off balance and off his feet. A figure appeared before him, eyes and teeth flashing in a savage grimace. A hard fist smashed into the older man's stomach. His wife screamed.

"Hey, Leroy, shut that honkey bitch's mouth."

"Right on, brother," Leroy replied gleefully, hurrying to where Louise Barr stood, eyes wide with terror, one fist held to her open, screaming mouth. The pink palm of a black hand crashed into her jaw, staggering her, the sound of the slap lost in the muffling silence of the falling snow.

"Shut yo' mouth, honkey bitch," Leroy commanded.

"In the car, Leroy. Put her in the car."

Leroy Jackson's eyes glowed with appreciation, anticipating what this turn of events would produce. "I can dig it, Sugar Man, I can *dig it*! That's righteous."

Cleavon Bates, alias Sugar Man, had obtained his street name from his precocious entry, at the age of thirteen, into the business of dealing drugs. A stretch at Lex, the federal drug rehabilitation center at Lexington, Kentucky, and his present parole, had removed him from his lucrative profession and lowered his means of livelihood to leading a gang of common muggers, not the most remunerative of occupations. Sugar Man felt sure that this time their efforts would pay off, that with this score they would strike it rich.

This dude and his woman dripped money. The furs, jewelry and cash would be nice. He even knew a place they could fence the three-year-old Continental. He turned his attention from Leroy, now busy struggling to shove the honkey broad into the back seat of the Lincoln, and began to thunder blows to the chest and stomach of their male victim.

Dr. Raymond Barr felt sharp new pain as each hard-knuckled fist hammered into his body. He cried out as bone let go while his ribs were repeatedly assaulted. He knew he was sustaining internal injuries, as well as the brutal bruising of his flesh. The detached, scientific portion of his mind told him he should call for help, but even as he opened his mouth to do so, another punch to the pit of his stomach drove the air from his lungs in a rasping *whoosh* that carried none of the volume necessary for a shout. Part of his expensive dinner came with it.

Sugar Man grunted in disgust, leaping backward and flipping his arm to rid his coat sleeve of the partially digested food. "Motherfucker puked on me," he growled, fitting tight leather gloves over his hands, their backs bulging from sewn-in plates of lead. Now, in retribution for the vomiting, Sugar Man turned his attention to Dr. Barr's head. Dr. Barr's agony became exquisite, blossoming into a pool of whirling lights . . . then into peaceful blackness.

"Dr. Barr . . . Dr. Barr, can you hear me?" a voice that rumbled like a gentle bear asked.

Raymond Barr opened his eyes to the horror of

his assault. He cringed back from the large black face looming over him, and raised one bandaged arm defensively. "No . . . oh, no. Please don't hit me again."

"No one's going to hurt you, Doctor," the black man said. "I'm Captain James Nero, Central Detective Division, Indianapolis police. If you're feeling up to it, I have some questions I must ask you."

Through partially open eyes, the tissue discolored with bruises, Dr. Barr examined this man at his bedside. Captain Nero wore a conservative gray, three-piece suit that had thin blue lines running vertically through the weave. It looked expensive and tasteful, not like the clothes of a mugger. Calming, the injured man opened his mouth and licked scabbed lips. His head was bandaged in white, which made the purple splotches around his eyes stand out even more, giving him a raccoon-like appearance. Struggling against rusty vocal cords, he spoke.

"M-my . . . my wife? Is . . . is she all right?"

Jim Nero frowned. He was unsure of how to break the news to this man. "I wish I could say yes. Or tell you anything definite. The truth is, we haven't found her as yet."

"K-kidnapping? Has there been any note? What are you doing to find her?"

"Not a kidnapping in the ordinary sense. She was taken from the parking lot, presumably in your Continental. That's where the trail ends. We haven't located the car . . . or her. I'm sorry."

Raymond Barr felt tears in his eyes. He made an effort to fight them back, wincing at the pain it caused. He turned his head aside a moment, lost in the horror of his beating.

"How long have I been here?"

"This is the second day since you were attacked. Now, I really must ask the questions. The doctors gave me only a few minutes. What can you tell me about the men who mugged you?"

Dr. Barr's face flushed dark with anger. "They were nigg—" He saw the glint in the black detective's eyes and amended his statement. "They were black. Three of them I know of."

"Can you describe them?"

"Two of them. The one who kept hitting me. He was big. I mean, real big: tall, thick shoulders, lots of muscles. And a mean, wild look in his eyes, like he hated everyone."

"What about the others?"

"Another guy held me from behind while the big one worked on me. This other man I saw was smaller, sort of skinny and . . . younger, I think. He's . . . he's the one who grabbed my wife . . . put Louise in the car."

"Did they say anything? Mention any names or where they were going?"

"Yes. Yes, they did. The big one called the other one, who took my wife, Leroy. And he, this Leroy, answered back to him as Sugar . . . Sugar something."

"Sugar Man?" Detective Nero's interest quickened.

"That's it."

"Ah. Sugar Man Bates. Well, well. We've been waiting to fall on that particular animal for a long time. Thank you, Doctor Barr. I know it's painful for you, but please try going over the events of that attack. I have to go now, but I'll be back and we'll be wanting chapter and verse on the assault." Captain Nero rose from his chair and crossed to the door. He paused, turning back. A wide, sincere smile creased his face.

"And don't worry, Doctor. We'll get those 'niggers' for you."

Chapter 2

CRIMINAL JUSTICE

Things began to warm up in Gulfport. As a result, Mark Hardin decided the time had come to remove Angie and the kids from what might suddenly become a combat zone. To make the departure less unhappy for all concerned, he decided on a trip to New Orleans.

Originally from the Crescent City, Angie had been a police officer there for several years. She and her children had not returned since her husband's death. Now, they reacted to the French Quarter like any tourists. Mark got them rooms at the Maison Toulouse on St. Peter Street and settled in for a two-day stay before Angie, Kevin, and Karen would return to Utah. On their first morning, over the strong coffee and delicious rolls of their complimentary continental breakfast in the lobby, Angie's eyes glowed with delight.

"Oh, Mark. I can't tell you what this trip has

meant to all of us. When we lived here, we . . . I suppose you'd say we took it all for granted. Are we really going to *tour* Jackson Square today?"

"Yeah. Then dinner at the Court of the Two Sisters, dancing at the Top of the Mart, and tomorrow we'll take a stern-wheeler up the Mississippi." Mark laughed sharply. "The last time *I* was in New Orleans . . . ah, forget it."

The last time the Penetrator had visited the shining Jewel of the South, he had slashed and shot his way through a counterfeiting ring, which had combined the most vicious and greedy of Dixie's underworld in a conspiracy with the would-be hemisphere conquerors of Communist Cuba. His results, and how he had achieved them, were nothing to recall over *croissants* and *café au lait*.

"Mark! Mark!" a shrill voice broke through their momentary silence. Kevin Dillon, dressed in an open collar shirt, shorts, and a windbreaker, with his bare feet shoved into Adidas running shoes, rushed into their secluded alcove, one of many in the hotel lobby. He stood with arms and legs akimbo. "Uh . . . I mean, *Mister* Hardin."

"Mark's all right with me," the Penetrator replied.

"Yeah, but Mom said . . ."

The two adults exchanged glances. Mark winked, wrinkling his nose. Angie shrugged. Kevin properly interpreted the byplay.

"Mark, then," he said through a spreading grin. "When are we gonna get some *real* breakfast? This stuff is the pits."

Mark laughed in spite of himself. "And what do you call a real breakfast?"

"There's a pancake house on the corner, I thought . . . I mean, maybe we can eat there, huh? An' have a strawberry waffle, an' country ham with red-eye gravy, an' eggs, an' . . ." It was obvious the boy had been studying the menu.

"Whoa! Slow down. You eat all that and you'll weigh three hundred pounds."

"No I won't, Mark. I'm hyper, you know that. Mom says that's why I bite my fingernails and jump around all the time and . . . like that." The boy suddenly realized that he was being kidded. Another infectious grin broke out. "*Awh.* You know what I mean."

"Okay, tiger. We'll go as soon as your mother and I finish. Where's Karen?"

"Dopey girls. You know? She's still upstairs picking out what she'll wear." Kevin turned away, content with the assurance of food soon to come. "See ya."

"My, oh my, how fast the time goes," Angie said with a sigh. "Having twins, I never gave thought to that old thing about little girls developing faster. Over the past year Karen has grown so *feminine.* She thinks of nothing but clothes and spends hours standing in front of a mirror. Her shape's changing; waist narrowing, legs filling out nicely, whether you noticed or not. Her breasts are developing too. Her periods started six months ago." Another sigh. "But Kevin? Kevie is still a little boy. He leaves his clothes strewn all over the house, sometimes he acts like he is allergic to soap and water, while his hair and appearance are matters of total indifference to him. Karen's stopped biting her nails, wants to use polish already. Kevin's incorrigible."

"Be thankful for small blessings. I've had a lot of older people tell me they never realized just how happy a home could be until the last small child grew up and left them . . . alone."

"Don't get maudlin on me, mister. We've got a lot of sightseeing to do."

Their tourist stint proved to be halcyon days of

intense joy that, instead of easing their departure, made it all the more difficult. Sad, lingering good-byes were said at New Orleans International, then Angie and the kids boarded a Braniff jet for Denver where they'd change planes for Salt Lake City. Mark flew his Mooney 201 back to Gulfport in a mood of dark contemplation. In his thoughts swam images of Angie and the twins. He thought, too, of the other Angie . . . dark, Latin-lovely Perez. A smart, competent private eye, a good cook and good company. Almost as good as Angie Dillon. Could it be, he wondered sourly, as the faces and possible future scenerios swirled in his consciousness, that I'm hung up on the name Angie? When he reached the hotel he wasted no time in breaking out his portable scrambler unit and calling the Stronghold.

"I've got a little something I want you to look up for me, Professor," Mark instructed after brief amenities.

"Of course, my boy. Anything you wish."

"Find out all you can about an outfit called Baymaster Ship Builders. It's a division of Armbrewster Steel and Iron Foundry in Indianapolis."

"This relates to that . . . ah, little matter?" Always cautious, Willard Haskins remained deliberately obscure even on a scrambler line.

"It does indeed. The hoods who are trying to persuade people to join the conglomerate seem to be mobbed up there. I figure to take a look at the place once I have some intel on the operation."

"Back to you at the usual time tomorrow, then. Any messages for anyone?"

"No." Mark's troubled thoughts crystallized in that instant on the Dillons; pert, lively, and lovely Angie; Karen, on the verge of womanhood and experiencing the first pangs of that change; Kevin, warm, lovable, and still filled with the world-wonder of a small boy. The ache intensified.

"No. No messages."

Raymond Barr was able to sit up most of the day when Detective Captain Jim Nero returned to his hospital room for the third time.

The bandages had been removed from Barr's face, leaving only a white gauze skullcap perched above his ears. The doctors had told him he had suffered a forty percent hearing loss that might or might not be permanent, and that one broken rib had slightly punctured a lung. *Like being only a little bit pregnant*, Barr thought around the pain and rose-tinted sputum he coughed up. But at least the bruises around his eyes, cheeks, and on his chest had faded to a sickly yellow-green and he no longer hurt *all* the time. He was even able to muster a smile of greeting when Nero entered.

"Well, Dr. Barr. You've proven that you scientists are tougher than you're given credit for. You look well on the way to mending." His voice changed, became softer, hesitant. "I'm sorry that the news I'm bringing isn't better suited to your mood."

"What's that?" Barr inquired, apprehension in his voice.

"We've found your wife . . ."

"She's . . . dead."

"Yes. I am sorry."

"I knew it. Expected it after a week went by. We're not rich, you know. I have only my salary from the chemical company I work for. With no ransom note . . . and not enough wealth to justify a kidnapping, I . . . I was sure. Was she . . . was . . . did they . . . ?"

Jim Nero's face gave Barr his answer in the way it seemed to melt into sadness even before he replied. "She was . . . criminally assaulted. Yes." He refrained from adding that she had been raped several times, over a period of two or more days, before finally being killed, her throat slashed from ear to ear.

"I do have some better news. We might recover your Mark Four and we have the three who did it in custody."

"That's . . . comforting. I don't mean about the car. I'm glad to hear you caught those bastards. When is their trial?"

Jim Nero looked uncomfortable. "Two of them are juveniles, you understand. A hearing is scheduled for them at Juvenile Court. Bates, the one they call Sugar Man, is nineteen and can be tried as an adult. The court hasn't set a date for that as yet. You'll be contacted by the DA's office. Now . . ." Nero reached under his coat, withdrawing a half-pint bottle of cognac. "I brought you some brandy. Remy-Martin, really quite good. I figured after what I had to tell you, you might want a hit."

Dr. Barr accepted the bottle thankfully. He poured a hefty three fingers into his water glass and downed it in a gulp. He smiled and nodded.

"I really am sorry about all this, Dr. Barr. Believe me, if there had been any way . . ." Nero left it unsaid, rising and extending his hand. "Good-bye, Doctor."

"Good-bye, Captain Nero. I'll see you at the trial."

Cleavon "Sugar Man" Bates would come to trial one month after Dr. Raymond Barr had been released from the hospital. Barr tried to adjust to life without Louise. He went three times a week to the cemetery where she lay under a shrinking mound of raw earth, haphazardly covered with squares of sod, still brown from winter's cold. He developed the habit of talking to his dead wife, telling her about his work, about the crocuses that were pushing their way early through the snow, of how lonely the

Thanksgiving and Christmas holidays had been without her. He even kept her up to date on progress in the cases against their assailants.

Leroy Jackson and Amos Petty, aged sixteen and seventeen respectively, had their appearance first, before Judge Banner of the Juvenile Court Division. They came with red-eyed, weeping mothers, dressed in their shabby best, faces solemn and manner contrite. They were, their attorneys pleaded, innocent victims. Cleavon Bates had done it all. They were terribly sorry about what had happened to that poor woman, but they'd had nothing to do with it. Raymond Barr's voice grew bitter as he described this scene to his deceased Louise.

Neither of the boys had thrown a punch at Dr. Barr, they protested. Barr's own testimony proved this to be true. Neither had taken anything from him or Mrs. Barr. Why, then, had Leroy put Mrs. Barr in the automobile? He had been afraid. Afraid of what Sugar Man would do to him if he didn't obey. They hadn't, they protested once again, touched a cent of the money that came from the victims or the sale of the stolen Lincoln. Nor any of the jewelry. One of the sobbing mothers, Dr. Barr was sure, wore Louise's watch on her arm, but he had no way of proving it. Once the main testimony was out of the way, character witnesses were paraded before the court.

Leroy and Amos were good boys, neighbors and local businessmen protested. They had unfortunately fallen in with bad company. Their antisocial behavior was the result of overreaction to a hostile white society, a black minister explained. They were, a black sociologist declared, victims themselves. The boys, misunderstood and culturally deprived products of the ghetto, should not be blamed for what society had forced them into.

It was society that was the villain. Everyone in

Indianapolis, in the United States, must be held to blame for the unfortunate death of Mrs. Barr and the loss of the Barr's property. Why, even though the car had not been recovered, didn't the pawnshop detail turn up Dr. Barr's Omega watch, his lodge ring, and wedding band? Surely these blameless boys could not be held responsible for the evil deeds of another.

Following this impassioned plea, the attorneys for Amos and Leroy delivered stirring summations. Society, they declared, picking up the sociologist's theme, should be on trial here, not these boys. It was time for a verdict.

In a soft tone, using the confused rhetoric of Juvenile Justice, liberal, kindly-hearted Judge Banner gave both boys two year's unsupervised probation, in the custody of their mothers. He admonished all present that ofttimes the real victims of a crime were its perpetrators. That these innocent children should be given an example of understanding, tolerance, and forgiveness seemed the only fair way. Leroy and Amos hugged each other in a frenzy of congratulations and strutted arrogantly out of the court.

In the hall, Leroy gave an exhibition of how deeply impressed he was with the need to amend his ways and live in rectitude. He flipped the bird at Dr. Barr. The unfortunate scientist's only hope of justice now rested in the trial of Cleavon Bates.

The first two days of the trial were taken up with jury selection. Dr. Barr, whose hearing never did recover, grew increasingly frustrated and eventually smoldered with repressed anger during this procedure. He only allowed his fury to lash out when describing the events at his wife's graveside. The defense attorney continuously challenged whites off the panel until the final jury consisted of five blacks, six white persons, and one woman Latina. Three days of testimony by police officers followed. Then Dr. Barr took the stand.

He did all right on direct examination. Then the smooth, talented defense attorney, who'd been appointed to the case by the court, and whose services came free to the defendant, went to work on Raymond Barr.

"You say that you saw this man, the defendant, Mr. Bates, standing before you, striking you with his fists?"

"That's correct."

"No doubt in your mind as to who it was hitting you?"

"None."

"Come now, Dr. Barr, it was late at night, you'd had a few drinks, it was snowing. This diagram here, the people's exhibit three, indicates you were parked some distance from any light source. Do you mean to tell me that in the dark, in the snow, your mind a little fuzzy from alcohol, in the confusing and terrifying circumstances of being attacked, you could positively identify this man's face?"

"I . . . yes. But I wasn't drunk . . . and I also heard one of them speak his name, then the police . . ."

"I didn't ask you if you heard his name, Doctor. I asked if you could positively identify the defendant by his face . . . ah, all things considered." The attorney looked knowingly at the jury.

"I . . . well, I . . . yes. Then the police told me . . ."

"The *police* told you *what*, Doctor? Did they come to your hospital room with a photograph of Cleavon Bates?"

"Yes."

"Did they say, 'We have this turkey, Bates, we've been trying to fall on for a long time. Don't you think, if you tried real hard, he might look a little like the man who attacked you?"

"No . . . no, it wasn't that way at all."

"Objection, Your Honor. Defense counsel is trying to put words in the witness's mouth. His approach is argumentative and not proper cross-examination."

"How's that?" the judge inquired.

"Counsel is attempting to imply by innuendo that Dr. Barr was intoxicated, when in fact he was sober. We stipulated that Dr. Barr had consumed a cocktail, had champagne with the meal. It was, after all, a celebration. The stipulation closes the door to further inquiry on cross. See Indiana Second at 146, 321, and 4322."

"Overruled on all points at issue. As you pointed out, this *is* cross-examination, Counsel. Mr. Silverstein must be allowed some latitude in the matter of impeaching one of your witnesses. And in seeking the facts."

"Then let the witness get the facts out."

"I've already ruled on your objection, Mr. Prosecutor. Jury is admonished to disregard any of this byplay. Now, continue, Mr. Silverstein."

"All right, Dr. Barr," Silverstein did a long, slow take. "*Doctor* . . . that's an honorary title, isn't it?"

Raymond Barr flushed. "It is not! I have a Ph.D. in biochemistry."

"I see," Silverstein sneered. "But you aren't a medical doctor, are you?"

"Your Honor," the prosecutor rose, arm above his head like a schoolboy seeking the teacher's attention. "What does this have to do with questioning the witness? With his reliability?"

"Is that in way of an objection, Counsel?"

"I'm merely trying to keep this trial on the right track, Your Honor. Defense counsel seems to have forgotten that means asking questions relating to facts in evidence."

"And I'm merely trying to determine how careful

and competent an observer Dr. Barr happens to be," Silverstein snapped.

"In that case, I'll allow the line of questioning to continue. But please try to connect it up, Counsel."

"Thank you, Your Honor."

So it went for the remainder of that day. Raymond Barr reached his wife's grave tired, morally and emotionally drained . . . and not a little drunk. He felt a sour foretaste of how the trial might end in this humiliating day of cross-examination. His smoldering anger grew hotter. Three days later the case went to the jury. After a two-hour deliberation, they returned a verdict.

Dr. Raymond Barr stood in open-mouthed shock beside the burly form of Detective Captain Jim Nero, his anger mounting, as the courtroom cleared. "What . . . what do they mean, not guilty on counts one and two of murder and kidnap? How can they do that?"

"Damn!" Nero growled. "I had him. I knew we had that Bates prick where we wanted him this time." His expression changed as he tried to make the best of it. "At least he fell on that GTA and possession and sale of stolen goods . . . if that's any consolation."

"And they call that justice? Justice for the criminal, all right."

Dr. Barr was to see another example of the workings of the liberal philosophy in the criminal justice system. A week later, curiosity—and a desire for even a modicum of vengeance—brought him to the courthouse for the sentencing of Sugar Man Bates.

Based on an enthusiastically glowing probation report made by the state, and a favorable parole record with the federal authorities, Bates was given three years probation. He was required to visit his probation officer twice monthly and to refrain from the company of known felons and persons of questionable reputation. That constituted the only punishment for the crimes he had committed. Bates managed to take it well.

Wearing a "Super Fly" suit of neon green, a pale puce shirt that sported a gigantic Peter Pan collar, and a leopard-skin cummerbund, Bates stood before the bench, grinning widely, nodding his head to an unheard melody and thanking the judge for being so compassionate. The judge dismissed Bates and his lawyer, remaining in his high-back leather swivel chair on the elevated platform of the bench.

Bates turned with an exaggerated, fluid slowness and began to walk out of the courtroom. As the now-freed mugger and murderer passed the aisle where Barr sat, he scowled darkly at the biochemist and continued his undulating way out through the swinging doors. Behind Bates's departing back, Raymond Barr listened with disbelief while the judge chatted with the prosecutor about a golf game they had scheduled that afternoon.

Raymond Barr didn't even try to staunch the flow of hot, bitter tears of rage and grief that ran down his cheeks as he explained to his dead Louise how the last of her murderer-rapists had been turned loose onto the streets to kill and maim again. The words cracked and broke as they came from his mouth. As he talked, anger and frustration turned to a cold, hateful conviction.

Dr. Raymond Barr had never thought of himself as a racist or a bigot. He had been raised in a proper liberal family, tolerant of all races and creeds. His schooling had followed this early inclination, giving him a feeling of oneness with all mankind and a burning conviction that rampant racism lay behind conservative demands for law and order and stiff penalties for offenders. Now, as he spilled out his rage and his newly forming plans to the unresponsive grass over his wife's grave, he found himself using the words of hate.

"The dirty niggers! They get defended at taxpayers' expense by fancy shyster lawyers and the bleeding-heart judges let off these murdering jigaboos with straight probation.

"They call it justice," he sobbed in anger. "Criminal justice! That's who benefits from it, all right. And the ones who administer it are just as criminal. But they'll pay. Yes, by God, if the corrupt courts won't punish animals like Bates, I'll get my own justice. Don't worry, Louise, I'll get revenge for you."

Chapter 3

EXECUTIVE DECISION

The Penetrator spent a totally unproductive week checking out the men he identified as regulars around the Baymaster shipyard. They came from everywhere: Chicago, Detroit, Cincinnati, Los Angeles. Some had minor records, others were entirely clean. All Mark knew was that they did no work at the yard and spent a lot of time around the offices of Bayside Fisheries, the conglomerate trying to wrest control of all independent fishing operations. So far, nothing had happened that was, strictly speaking, illegal.

But the problem intrigued Mark. He knew the smell of corruption, could sense the heavy-handed feel of a full-bore crooked scam in the making, yet each day passed with nothing being done on Bayside's part outside the law. Then Mark met Junior Jones.

Junior had been a fisherman since the age of nine.

He'd shrimped with his father and grandfather, later with an older brother. At last, on his own, he ran one boat while making payments on a second, the keel of which he'd ordered laid. Now, in his late forties, he owned a warehouse, and a processing plant for fish, crab, oysters, and shrimp. He also had a retail sales outlet, shipped direct to restaurants as far removed as Chicago and, from his desk, captained a fleet of shrimpers, led to sea by his eldest son. He came from typical tidewater Mississippi stock, hard as the nine-gauge plate that made the hull of his newest fishing boat, stubborn, proud, red-necked, and staunchly WASP. He weighed people in an instant and acted toward them according to his own lights.

"Now, why the hell didn't you come to me in the first place? I'm the biggest holdout against those bastards, so I oughta know what it's all about, right?"

The Penetrator forced a deprecating smile and trotted out his cover story. "Well, frankly, I've been interested in Bayside as an investment possibility. It wasn't until recently that I began hearing some . . . unsettling things about them. That's why I decided to talk to someone who doesn't find them the most desirable thing around."

"Bullshit! You've been pokin' around here, nosin' into things for more'n a month now. Went away for awhile, then came back. What is it you're really after. You one of Bayside's hard men? You're big enough for it."

Mark made a quick reevaluation of this crusty, barrel-chested ex-fisherman. "Okay, Junior, I'll level with you. There's a mighty big stink rising from Bayside . . . and I don't mean rotten fish. I get the feeling they're into something illegal, like pressuring people to join them. But I can't put a name to it. No one seems willing to talk."

Junior eyed Mark suspiciously. "You one of those government men? Somethin' about antitrust, like that?"

"Nope."

"Okay. Then ask your questions and I'll answer those I can."

"Those you can or those you *will*?"

Junior snorted and lighted a cigar. "Smart-ass."

"What's the connection between Baymaster and Bayside?"

"Bay*master* . . . Bay*side* . . . all the same kettle of fish. Also Bay*shore* Seafood Products and a bunch more. What they want is to control the whole kit and caboodle. They want to own the boats that make the catches, the plants that process them, the distributors . . . everything."

"That verifies what I've learned so far. What I can't understand is, given the people who seem to be involved, why haven't they gone in for any rough stuff?"

"Oh, they have, they have. Only folks around here aren't given to talking a lot about their troubles . . . particularly to outsiders. Give me two days time and I'll have something solid for you."

The Penetrator shrugged mentally. He'd wasted the better part of two months now, feeling all the while he was on a wild goose chase, so he might as well spend a few more days. "Okay with me. I'll see you day after tomorrow."

Joseph T. Armbrewster sat behind the modest expanse of his four-foot by thirty-inch mahogany veneer desk. He had not become a multi-millionaire by frivolously wasting money on gaudy, expensive office furniture. The top of the desk, highly polished and protected by a sheet of glass, was uncluttered. In the *In* box, the day's mail, opened and screened by his secretary, awaited his attention. The only adornment was a gold-edged, double-fold picture frame.

From behind the three glass panels of the frame, photos of a young girl looked out at the busy industrialist. From left to right they depicted different ages in the life of a honey-blonde, slightly freckled, blue-eyed child. The most recent one showed her at about fifteen. Armbrewster looked up from the file folder he studied with great concentration, and sighed heavily as his eyes brushed past the portraits.

"If only there had been some other way," he thought for the millionth time. "If only we'd known in time." He returned his attention to a collection of newspaper clippings in the Manila folder.

The first item, a brief third of a column from an inside page, reported the savage beating of Dr. Raymond Barr, biochemist and toxicologist for Croydon Chemical Company. Armbrewster reread it for the tenth time, eyes glowing with a special hatred as he devoured the words. The next article covered the discovery of Mrs. Barr's body. The one following dealt with the juvenile hearing of two, unnamed youths and their release on two years' unsupervised probation. Again, Dr. Barr's name figured prominently in the story. The last clipping gave an account of the trial and sentencing of one Cleavon "Sugar Man" Bates.

Stress lines of anger appeared around Armbrewster's eyes as he read, and his thick, work-muscled fingers closed into fists, the knuckles whitening from the intensity of his feelings. His gaze moved on down the double columns until a growl of raw fury rumbled deep in his throat.

"Coons again! Goddamned garbage spewing out to pollute our cities." Setting the file aside, Armbrewster keyed an intercom switch. "Send in Dr. Barr, will you please?"

Dr. Raymond Barr looked even more diminutive

than his five-foot-seven-inch, slender frame could account for as he entered the large office with its smaller-than-usual desk and floor-to-ceiling bookshelves. He crossed to a chair indicated by a wave of his host's hand and seated himself. The discoloration from his injuries had dissipated over the time since the mugging, leaving only a little scar tissue under one eye. But his hearing had not recovered, its loss in one ear now pronounced permanent, two months after the attack. The only outward sign of his ordeal was a slight trembling of his hands.

That, along with his partial deafness and a growing dependence on alcohol, had cost him his job at Croydon. He hadn't any idea why he'd been summoned to the headquarters of Armbrewster Steel and Iron Foundry. His summary dismissal from Croydon and a growing obsessive hatred of blacks had blinded him to any career ambitions, in addition to the realities of his life. His mind, then, was entirely blank as he silently studied Joseph T. Armbrewster.

Armbrewster was a huge man, thick-shouldered and still well-muscled, despite his fifty-seven years. He had started in the steel business as a puddler, working the hot floor of the mill, sweating and fighting his way to foreman, then on to the top. A self-made man. Cold gray eyes, as hard and colorless as his major product, looked out from under bushy brows of salt-and-pepper hue. A thick thatch of wiry hair hung over his brow and bristled around his ears, one of which showed the puffy swelling of many bare-knuckle confrontations. His chest was big, but his belly remained flat, and hard, narrowing to a trim waist, unseen behind the desk. When he smiled, with just the right touch of sympathy in his expression, he revealed large, white teeth, all his own.

"Dr. Barr. Let me express my sincerest sympathy for your recent loss."

"Thank you, Mr. Armbrewster. But, surely you didn't call me here for that."

Armbrewster changed, became affable. "No. Naturally not. And . . . call me Joe. Only time anyone ever called me *Mister* and I couldn't do anything about it was when I shipped out with the Coast Guard for two years." He lowered his voice. "I understand we share a mutual enemy."

"I beg your pardon? My hearing, you know."

"Quite right. A little present from those niggers who mugged you and murdered your wife."

Raymond Barr paled, then flushed with rising anger. Any mention or thought of what had happened to his darling Louise drove him to the edge of frenzy. His eyes glazed with hate and the trembling of his hands increased. Before he could make a reply, Armbrewster continued.

"Gently, gently, my friend. You see, I know what you are feeling right now. Know the heartache and anguish. I, too, have experienced tragedy at the hands of those . . . *beasts*."

"H-how is that?" Dr. Barr felt amazement . . . and the beginning of hope. Here was a kindred soul, someone who had endured the unendurable. He looked up, soft brown, tear-filled eyes locking on the steely orbs opposite him.

Joe Armbrewster reached out, turning the three-panel picture frame. "My daughter. A lovely child. So brilliant, sparkling. Our only child. My . . . wife and I were quite open-minded about things. We . . . sent her to the public schools. The *integrated* public schools. Things went quite well all right until she reached Junior High. She . . . she met a boy. Raved about him, but never would bring him home. Then her personality seemed to change. She lost weight, became surly and suspicious.

"We . . . found out later that her 'friend' had turned her on to drugs. He was, of course," Armbrewster sighed heavily, "a nigger. When she was fifteen," his thick left index finger indicated the right-hand photo, "not long after this was taken, she ran away to live with him. This . . . this drug-peddling monster! We didn't hear from her for several months. Since she was underage, the police looked for her, but not all that hard. So many runaways these days . . . and with all the propaganda, her situation not all that unique. Then one night she called. She talked with my wife and I. She was . . . pregnant.

"That's the last time we heard from her." Armbrewster appeared drained, sunken in upon himself. "Two days later the police notified us to come claim her body. She'd died of a heroin overdose. There'd . . . there'd been a big party that her pusher-lover threw to celebrate his expected child. Stacey . . . my daughter . . . got hold of some nearly pure stuff. It killed her."

A peculiar light of horror suffused Raymond Barr's features. Here was a story every bit as tragic as his own. He couldn't help but ask the question, though his own experience made him feel he knew the answer.

"What was done about it?"

"Nothing. When the police came, the drugs were all gone. Her . . . uh, boyfriend . . . had decamped. There was no proof as to how and from whom she had obtained the narcotics."

"What has this to do with me?"

"I'll answer that by asking a question. Do you believe in the Biblical injunction: 'Vengeance is mine, saith the Lord'?"

Barr's glance wavered to the desk top. "I . . . I've never been much of a religious man, Joe."

"Nor have I. But there is one line in the Bible I

do know and fully endorse: 'An eye for an eye and a tooth for a tooth.' And that's the reason I asked you here."

"This is because of, as you put it, our mutual tragedy?"

"Precisely. That what befell us is mutual, is not by the wildest, random coincidence. It happens in the same way every day. Are you aware that a twenty-percent segment of our population is responsible for seventy-eight percent of the crime but that they constitute only forty-seven percent of those arrested for serious crimes and only thirty-eight percent of those confined in prisons or jails? Check it out. That comes from the FBI's Uniform Crime Report. I've been thinking about this for five years now and I've come to a conclusion.

"I don't want to just get revenge on the animals who attacked you and your wife, or the scummy little coon pusher who was responsible for what happened to Stacey and for sending my wife to a mental institution. I want to get them all. Every nigger bum who escapes punishment for the crimes he commits, must somehow be made to pay."

Shocked at Armbrewster's sudden vehemence, Raymond Barr leaned back in his chair, his attaché case held almost defensively before him. "How . . . how do I figure into this plan for revenge?"

"You, sir, are a biochemist and toxicologist. Doesn't that suggest something to you?"

"I can understand getting even with those who hurt us. But . . ." Surprise over the casual manner in which Armbrewster had revealed his idea had faded away. Gone too was any realization that it was the fault of the ultraliberal court system, which considered the rights of a criminal superior to the rights of the victim, that his wife's killers had gone unpunished. In his mind now, Raymond Barr saw visions of himself kneeling at his wife's graveside, promising her, vowing before God, to get vengeance—not only on those who had killed her, but on all blacks. But that was an unsound idea, a wild fantasy born of grief and frustration that he had quickly rejected, chiding himself for such unhealthy thinking. But now . . . first he must be certain, needed to be absolutely sure Armbrewster meant what he said.

Armbrewster looked saddened, his replying words were hesitant. "I thought in you I had found a kindred mind, a will as solidly forged as my own to the utterly necessary extermination of these vermin. Perhaps . . . I was wrong?"

"Your . . . your statement came as a surprise, is all, Joe," Barr said, remaining cautious. "Please go on."

"You are a scientist. You are accustomed to developing various substances. I am a man of considerable wealth. Together we can achieve a way of accomplishing what other means, legal means, have failed to do.

"I'll put it another way. What would you do, Dr. Barr, if given the opportunity to avenge yourself on the animals who murdered your wife and beat you mercilessly, *and not stand any chance of being found responsible for it*?"

Barr had no difficulty in answering the question. "I . . . I'd devote the rest of my life to such a project."

"And you are currently unemployed?" To Barr's affirmative nod, Armbrewster continued. "If you had unlimited funds and a private laboratory, isolated from outside interferences, what could you develop?"

"That depends on what you are looking for."

"What I want is some chemical, or organism—and a method of spreading it undetected—that will be selective in its effect. I'll pay a bonus of five million dollars if you can produce a means of insuring, exclusive of any harm to all others, the death of every black who has committed a crime and gone unpunished for it."

Raymond Barr's head throbbed. He could hardly believe what he had heard. Here were the means for fulfillment of his vow, along with a tidy profit, if Armbrewster could be trusted. He felt the need of a hefty drink to steady his nerves, channel his thinking. What could he say, some proof of his ability, to make sure Armbrewster could go through with it? Then he had it.

"There is a rare blood disease, one of the many things that distinguishes the difference between blacks and whites. It is called sickle-cell anemia. Only blacks can get it. They, or those of mixed genetic background. It destroys the red blood cells. The platelets, under a microscope, look as though something had taken a large crescent bite out of them, leaving a sickle-shaped portion behind. Obviously, these damaged cells can no longer carry a sufficient oxygen supply to the body and brain.

"Normally, only a few are afflicted with this debilitating illness, and most prevalently those living in areas with an altitude in excess of five thousand feet. But if I were able to find a means for accelerating the incidence of sickle-cell anemia and the rate of degeneracy for the red corpuscles, we could look forward to nearly one hundred percent efficiency within a year or two after initial tests."

"I want it done a hell of a lot sooner than that. Stacey's been dead five years now, and this thing has grown in me like . . . like a cancer. Then my wife was driven insane by grief and an inability to reconcile the truth with her previous beliefs. I *have* no more time! Results within months would be more like it."

Dr. Barr allowed himself a small smile. "Given

the proper facilities and staff—and unlimited money—I think I could guarantee you that."

Armbrewster's mood changed entirely, became affable and confidential. "Dr. Barr, it's only fair for me to inform you that I had a complete background investigation conducted on you. I'll admit I was most impressed with your reputation as a genius in your chosen field. However, I must confess I never suspected that you could so quickly and easily get to the heart of the problem and give me the solution I seek."

Dr. Barr raised a cautionary hand. "I can't guarantee that this particular theory will work. We may have to try a dozen approaches and ten times that number of genetic test combinations before the end is in sight."

"'No matter. What is it you'll need?"

"Some sturdy building, lots of windows, maybe thirty by forty feet in size. Water and electric facilities, of course. And remote, as you suggested. Within a week I can give you a complete list of equipment and supplies needed for the laboratory. Now, as to assistants . . ."

"Wouldn't they be a liability, considering what we're going to do?"

"No. Not at all. They can be told that we are . . ."—smile lines crinkled around Barr's eyes—"working on a *cure* for SCA. A nice touch, don't you think? Three would do nicely. Not too well-advanced in experience or training, certainly. That way we can be sure they will never put together what we're producing.

"Then, too, the lab will have to be close to some area where I have ready access to blood from blacks and their bone marrow."

"What about Puerto Rico? I have several large tracts of land there. One of the places has a cement block warehouse on it about the size you need."

"Fine. We're agreed then? I'd . . . I'd about despaired of ever finding anyone who could understand how I felt."

"You did read that list off as though you had given it considerable thought."

"I have dreamed of nothing else since the day I watched those craven scum walk out of the courtroom as free as the air."

Armbrewster rose from behind his desk, extending a hand. The two men shook earnestly. "Well then, partner, we're about to launch a great enterprise. Don't let those dreams trouble you further. Think instead of the magnificent contribution you are about to make to mankind."

Chapter 4

LABORATORY OF EVIL

Dr. Raymond Barr leaned back into the high, curved back of the rattan chair. He smacked his lips in appreciation of the *piña colada*, liberally laced with 151-proof rum. Looking about the room, at its South Sea decor, his pleasure dimmed slightly. It was all rather fakey.

But then, tourists were tourists, and neither Maude nor Percy from Hammondsport could tell there was a difference between Caribbean and Tahitian. What they wanted was romance and a hint of adventure. The detached cabanas on the beachfront at the *Nacional de San Juan* provided that.

Armbrewster's wealth had opened doors to luxury and a life-style unknown to the small biochemist. He really should, he reminded himself, work harder at enjoying this brief stay in San Juan. Before long the lab equipment and supplies would arrive and he would be hard at work. He took another long pull on the pineapple-coconut-flavored drink, wondering what Joseph T. Armbrewster might be doing at that moment. Never mind, he thought. Whatever it would be it couldn't be as pleasant as this.

Joe Armbrewster had hardly settled himself behind his desk, following his usual morning tour of the foundry floor, when the intercom buzzed.

"Yes?"

"A call on line two, Mr. Armbrewster. Jennings at Baymaster in Gulfport."

"Thank you, Shirley. I'll take it." Armbrewster lifted the receiver and punched the blinking button. "Yeah?"

"Mr. Armbrewster, we've got some problems down here. Some guy's stickin' his nose in our business."

"Nothing you can't handle, is it, Ted? This isn't an official inquiry, is it? I mean, there's nothing illegal in what we're doing . . . technically, that is." To the long, pointed pause, he added with a note of irritation, "Well, is there?"

"I don't know about the big business side of it, Mr. Armbrewster. If you say this conglomerate thing doesn't violate antitrust, then I'll go along. But . . . some of those boys you've sent down to get things organized . . . well . . ."

"Well, what? They're getting results, aren't they?"

"Sure, sure. It's the methods they're using that I'm wondering about."

"I don't follow you, Ted."

"The other night, ah, a couple of the holdouts had their boats burned to the water line."

"So?"

"What I mean is, if that sort of thing got out, we could be in a lot of trouble."

"Look, Ted. Business is tough and dirty. You can't come out on top without being just a little tougher and dirtier than your competition. What difference does it make so long as they get things to go our way? You can't make an omelet without breaking some eggs. Napoleon said that."

"I don't know any Napoleon, but I do know we're in deep shit if the law finds out about guys breakin' heads and burnin' boats."

Armbrewster's voice grew cold. "You want me to send someone else down to take your place, Ted? Think a little vacation might do you some good?"

"No. No, sir. Nothing like that. I just wanted to clear this with you, make sure everything was like you wanted."

"The boys are doing their jobs. That's what I hired them for. That's all you need to know . . . and that's all I want to hear."

"Yes, sir."

"Fine, Ted. I hope to hear you have this thing sewed up within the next two weeks. Good-bye."

Heat and humidity played hell with a load of rum, Dr. Barr thought as he stumbled on a slight rise in the ground outside a large cement block building. So this was to be his laboratory, eh? Off in the forest of Puerto Rico. Couldn't rightly call it a jungle, but it was the next thing to it. Wiping sweat from his brow, Raymond Barr entered the structure through a small personnel door.

"Ah. *Buenas dias, Señores,*" he greeted the workmen in poor, textbook Spanish.

The workmen, who were shoveling accumulated refuse into a wheeled metal bin, looked up but didn't make any reply. Their eyes flickered with a barely suppressed hatred. Like many Puerto Ricans, they didn't like *gringos* and made no effort to disguise this fact. *¡Puerto Rico Libre*! was more than a slogan shouted by leftist students. Still silent, the men returned to their labors. For his own part, Dr. Barr tried to cover the affront by dissembling.

"So, this is to be my laboratory," he said aloud, speaking his earlier thought. "Most adequate, I'd say. Don't you think?" he asked no one in particular, but as he turned his head he could almost swear that he saw the slightest flicker of motion as Louise passed by. Blinking, he licked suddenly dry lips. Damn! He'd never realized that rum, so subtle on the palate, could hit him so hard. But thinking of liquor made him thirsty again. He was glad he had the forethought to bring along a thermos of chilled pineapple juice and that marvelous Silver Label Bacardi that wasn't even available in the States. Hurrying outside, he headed for his rented car.

After slaking his thirst, Raymond Barr cast a reproachful look at the lab building. Surly bunch of devils, he thought of the workmen. Did everyone on this blasted island have a taint of black blood? God, they're taking over the world! Good thing the supplies wouldn't arrive for two more days. They'd probably steal him blind. Criminality, Dr. Barr was coming to believe in his increasingly confused mind, had to be as much a part of the Negro gene pool as sickle-cell anemia. He returned the thermos to the car and headed toward the distant beach.

Nestled among the trees, a hundred yards above the high tide line, Barr found the small cottage he would occupy once the lab went into operation. He climbed the two sagging steps to a narrow porch and reached for the doorknob.

"Hey, man, you the new dude we heard about movin' in here?" came a laconic voice from the distant corner of the building, halting Dr. Barr's action.

"Who . . . who are you?" Dr. Barr asked, studying a lanky man in his mid-twenties, barefoot and bearded, wearing faded khaki cutoffs and a tank top. Gaunt cheeks and deep-set eyes were highlighted by a halo of fuzzy, light brown hair. The scientist's inspection halted at the eyes. They were haunting, commanding, like the eyes of . . . *of Charles Manson*, the name supplied itself from Dr. Barr's memory.

"I'm Lessor . . . Brad Lessor. Me 'n' my family live over the hill there. We're your only neighbors."

"Your family?"

"Yeah. The Scum of the Earth." Lessor laughed, a hollow, mocking sound. "That's what we call ourselves. We've got this little commune, see? We chucked society and all its hassles to come down here to do what we could for our brothers and sisters who are struggling against the fascist establishment."

Dr. Raymond Barr shuddered visibly. An epithet flashed through his mind, to be quickly suppressed by the realization that this was indeed his only neighbor. Wouldn't do to make the locals hostile . . . any more so than the average Puerto Rican seemed to be, that is. Dr. Barr tried to work up a smile.

"Well, Mr. . . . ah, Lessor. I'm, ah, I'm Raymond Barr. *Doctor* Barr. I'm a research scientist and I'll be working in the old warehouse west of here."

"Armbrewster's? Not like that capitalist pig to be so generous for the sake of research." Lessor's vocabulary told Dr. Barr that the young man had a better mind and education than his appearance attested to. He decided to make the most of it.

"We're also, ah, working to better the lives of our . . . black brothers." Barr's throat tasted of bile at his use of the words. "Research into sickle-cell anemia."

A mischievous light flared in Lessor's eyes. "To cure it . . . or to cause it?"

Dr. Barr blanched. My God, did the whole world

know? He started to stammer a reply, but Lessor beat him to it.

"I don't really give a shit which. Only a joke, you know? So it was in bad taste. That's what the Scum are all about. Bad Taste, in capital letters. Besides, we're into radical politics, not race. I'll buy you a drink."

The magic words! Barr's face brightened with acceptance. "Nicest thing I've heard all day. The workmen over there wouldn't even speak to me. But . . . I, ah, haven't, ah, moved in as yet. No means for hospitality."

"C'mon over to the commune. The booze is on me. And a little grass if you've a mind to."

The liquor turned out to be vinegary red table wine of an inferior local brand. But the marijuana was first class. Dr. Barr had never blown weed before, but a little instruction by Lessor and he began toking like an expert. The sensation puzzled him at first, then he relaxed into the chemical high it produced. Twice he caught himself talking to Louise as though she were actually there beside him. He covered his lapses with what he hoped would be success and nodded pleasantly through the afternoon heat. Mostly, he enjoyed the scenery.

Lessor had many female followers. They wore little or nothing in the way of clothing and the flock of children all ran naked as the sky. Dr. Barr had been celibate since his wife's death and now noticed a growing insistence in his loins as he eyed the parade of feminine flesh . . . young flesh at that. One girl in particular, she couldn't be more than sixteen, caught his attention.

She constantly contrived to come within his range of vision. She wore only a tight, wraparound skirt, slung low on her hips, and an inviting smile. As she walked, her slim, deeply tanned body undulated provocatively and her small, firm breasts swayed with the movement. The last time she came past, she was leading a gaggle of ten naked youngsters, ranging from toddlers to a pair of skinny nine-year-olds, toward the distant beach for a swim. She was as bare-assed as they. Dr. Barr discovered, much to his discomfort, that he had a painfully engorged erection.

"What ya' see, if ya' like, you can have," Lessor said with sudden, expansive generosity. "I've decided to make you an honorary member of the tribe, Doc. You want a little tail off that sweet thing, you've got it. It's obvious she has the hots for you. What say? Wanna stay the night?"

All of Dr. Raymond Barr's staid conventions crumbled in the memory of his momentary glimpse of sparsely haired pubic triangle. Licking his lips, he reached for the wine jug, gulped down a throat-working swallow and made a face.

"You're on, Brad, you're on. And tomorrow I'll bring some better quality liquor. That stuff should be labeled hazardous to your health. Now, there's a little business proposition I'd like to discuss with you."

"What's that?"

"I don't think I can trust those workmen sent out from town. I'm going to need someone around whose . . . of my own race. What would you say to becoming the general caretaker, foreman if you like, of the cottage grounds and the lab? I'd see you and your, ah, tribe are well paid for your services and you'd not need to work more than two or three days a week."

"Level with me, Doc. Are you really that much in love with the jigs?"

Booze and marijuana were having a profound effect on Dr. Barr. He grinned like a kid with a key to the candy store. "You kidding? I hate the lousy bastards. But . . . but what I'm doing has to be kept a secret. You understand?"

"Sure, sure. Just what is it?"

"Like I told you, I'm doing research into sickle-cell anemia. I'm going to need a steady and reliable supply of black blood and bone marrow. Do you think you can arrange that?" Had he been sober, Dr. Barr would never have been so frank at this stage of his acquaintance with Brad Lessor. As the situation stood, though, he had lost all inhibitions. Mostly his body burned and ached to lie with that lovely young girl with the raven hair. He had enough control, however, to insist that business come first.

"No sweat on that, Doc. We'll get you all you need. Don't let that 'love your black brothers' crap fool you. That's just a scam to let us stay here with no hassles. You see, I've got this dream I want to make come true."

"How's that?"

"You know as well as I do that sooner or later there's gonna be a big race war. The way I have it figured, our government's gonna let the niggers win." Lessor shrugged, extending one hand and crumpling the fingers together, making a falling gesture with his arm. "After that, everything's going to hell. The spades'll not be able to keep up with the technology they've seized. They lack initiative . . . it's their slave mentality. They'll have to come looking for some white dude to lead them. I intend to be that man. Me an' the Scum of the Earth. Far out, huh?"

"Somewhat." Dr. Barr took a drag on the joint Lessor handed him. "It's settled then? Good." He rose, beginning to tug off his shirt, eyes already tracking the distance where the teen-aged temptress had disappeared toward the sea.

Mark Hardin gained admittance to Junior Jones's office the moment he arrived. Jones looked agitated, his emotions as bristly as the small mustache that graced his upper lip.

"I don't know who you are or whatever the hell you can do about this thing, but something's gotta be done and damn fast," he said without preamble.

"I don't think I'm tracking with you, Junior."

"Three of these goddamned Chicago hood types were seen on the docks the other night, just before Obie's and Chet's boats were burned. This Bayside thing is gettin' rough."

"Do the police know this?"

"The cops, my ass! They say that's not proof of anything. That these three guys were all in a poker game at the Baymaster shipyard when the fire started. Shit. I don't give a damn what anyone says, this cartel is illegal. An' now they're using muscle to get their way. More than a few threats, can't you see?"

"I'm sorry, but there's nothing I can do. Not directly, that is." Mark regretted having to put off Junior Jones like that. He had come to like the man and respect him for his stand against the fishing conglomerate that was being formed. But it wouldn't do for anyone to get the idea that he could or would do anything to revenge illegal acts.

"*Awh*, hell, you're just like all the others. What's this 'not directly' you're talking about?"

"I can pass along everything to other, interested, parties and maybe they will do something."

"Fine. Just great. Suppose you do that . . . but don't come back here until something is done. Now get outta here, I'm busy."

Mark suppressed the reply he would have liked to make, leaving the office without another word.

Outside Junior's office, lounging against a pair of tall wooden bollards on the fishy-smelling dock, two men watched the Penetrator's progress. As Mark walked out of sight of the Jones Seafood Co-op building, they came alert and turned as one, following after him quickly.

Halfway down the pier, one of the men called aloud. "Hey you! Big boy. We wanna talk to you."

The Penetrator stopped, turned slowly, already weighing the situation. He faced two men he had previously identified as members of the Bayside Fisheries corporation security force. Junior was right. They did look like Chicago hoods.

"What do you want?"

"You been asking the wrong questions about the wrong company in too many places. We're supposed to bring you a message."

"What's that?"

Before answering, the talkative one brought a spring-loaded lead sap out of a rear trouser pocket. His partner withdrew a pair of brass knuckles from his jacket and fitted them on one ham-sized fist.

"This!" the sap wielder shouted. Then they both rushed their intended victim.

Chapter 5

QUALIFIED SUCCESS

They chose a bad tactic. It was the sort of thing street brawlers specialized in, or men who only faced thoroughly cowed suckers who were in over their heads to a loan shark. To their regret, they discovered it wasn't the sort of thing one did to the Penetrator.

As their rush neared him, Mark faded back with his right foot, deciding to take out the blabbermouth with the sap first. When the range closed to just the right point, the Penetrator pivoted toward him, bending far backward and snapping his coiled right leg forward, the hard leather in front of his shoe heel making contact with the thug's kneecap. The beefy man yowled in pain, dropped his blackjack, and crashed to one side. Rolling over, he tried to stand, forgetting for a moment his injury and putting his full weight on the bad leg. He tottered to the edge of the pier and, shrieking, fell into the water twelve feet below. Mark directed his attentions to the other hood.

The guy with the knuckle-duster came in low, shoulders rolling like a boxer. He snapped a straight jab at Mark's jaw, putting enough weight behind it to break bone. But the protruding face was no longer there. The Penetrator had made a sweeping, graceful pivot back and to the right. As the "security man" followed his own momentum, Mark crossed his arms and drove upward in a rising "A" block.

As soon as he made contact, Mark folded the brass-weighted hand into a "chicken wing," bending down and backward while his opponent's running feet carried his lower body out from under the top. The hood smashed to the heavy planks of the pier head first with a hollow-melon sound. Almost too easy, the Penetrator thought, as he knelt beside the stunned man. His right hand was folded into a wedge, poised to strike at the other man's larynx and kill if necessary. Slowly the eyes Mark studied regained focus. The man moaned.

"Sonny boy, the next time your boss sends someone after me, he'd better make sure it's a *man*. Your hard-guy days in Gulfport are over. Pack your bags and get out of town."

The hood glared his anger, seeking to rise, then flinched at the fury in the Penetrator's eyes. "Don't bad-mouth me, you son-of-a-bitch," the gunman growled. "There's more of us than there is of you. We got your number and we'll feed you to the fish in little pieces if you don't haul your butt outta here."

"Look, asshole. Go pluck that turkey you're with out of the water and make tracks back to Delaney Street before I reassemble you both as a quartet of midgets."

The Chicago tough guy's eyes had widened at

Mark's use of the familiar cop phrases. "You the heat?" They had strict orders not to cross the local law.

"I'm more heat than you've ever felt, chump." Mark reached into a jacket pocket and withdrew a two-inch sliver of blue flint shaved into a Cheyenne arrowpoint. He dropped it on the hood's chest. "You've got a choice. You and your crew can leave town upright . . . or stay in boxes."

"Christ! You . . . you're the P-Penetrator?"

Mark's smile was intense and wintery. "*Now* you get the picture." His voice became scornful. "Who hired this collection of so-called heavy talent?"

"I . . . we . . . work for Bayside Fisheries. That's all I know. Guy named Ted Jennings honchoes this end of the business. Honest, that's all I know to give you."

His voice heavy with sarcasm, the Penetrator commented, "I wonder if they know how badly they're being ripped off? Okay. So you win a free walk this time. If you or any of your half-ass mob shows a face around here again, I'll feed you your balls for breakfast. You might be hell on wheels in Chicago, but you're out of your class here. On your feet!" he commanded, rising smoothly, jerking the hefty hood along by his injured wrist. Mark gave him the bum's rush to the edge of the pier, hurling the thoroughly subdued tough guy out into the air to hang a frightful second before plunging beneath the green, oil-scummed waves below.

Ten minutes later the Penetrator parked his rental car half a block from the main offices of Bayside Fisheries. The conglomerate, the idea even of a multinational entity for that matter, wasn't necessarily an evil that would send the Penetrator into combat. But there had been heads thumped, bones broken, and now two fishing boats burned to the waterline. Whatever their goal, businesswise, their methods of achieving that end had a distinctly criminal flavor to them. The Bayside Fisheries conglomerate was connected to Baymaster Ship Building, which was listed as a subsidiary of Armbrewster Steel in Indiana.

From there, according to Professor Haskins's report, the Armbrewster industrial octopus spread out to several foreign nations, as well as Stateside and to Puerto Rico. What possible advantage could Armbrewster find in bludgeoning the Gulf Coast fishing industry into line? But then, like many other wealthy and powerful men, perhaps Armbrewster found his achievements only made him thirst for more wealth, more power. Maybe a good cage-rattling would suffice to bring Bayside and its far-removed head back into line with what was laughingly called "acceptable" business ethics. Abandoning his thoughts, Mark quickly entered the building.

Bayside had selected the tallest building in town, the Hilton, for its headquarters. This afforded them a view of the dock area and the highway that connected Biloxi on the east with New Orleans some hundred miles distant to the west. Riding up in the elevator, Mark worked himself into the same tough-guy role he had used with the hoods sent to discourage him with a few lumps.

"Yes, sir. May I help you?" a pert, attractive receptionist asked when Mark entered the office.

"I'd like to see Mr. Jennings."

"Your name, please?"

"Tell him there's a very angry citizen out here waiting to shove a fist down his throat if he isn't out here in five seconds. I don't like getting pushed around by his goons."

The girl looked entirely flustered, her mouth working but nothing coming out. She darted a nervous glance at a cluster of men to one side. One of the trio lounging at the table behind and to the left of the Penetrator pushed away from his chair and began a rolling walk that went well with his broad shoulders and thick legs. His growling voice fit the bear-like physique.

"You! The one with the mouth. The lady asked for your name. You gonna give it or am I gonna toss you outta here on your ass?"

"Besides, Mr. Jennings isn't here, no one is," the girl squeaked as the hulking figure closed on the Penetrator.

"Ya hear that, turkey? Nobody home. So butt out, right?" He extended a thick-wristed hand to shove a fat finger into Mark Hardin's chest.

"Wrong," the Penetrator said quietly, locking onto the other man's arm and bending the wrist painfully backward. Up on tiptoes now, the security man released a bellow of rage and pain as he tried to launch himself toward his adversary.

The Penetrator took advantage of this momentum to execute his next move, swinging the bulky hood like a pendulum, releasing him so he flew into the other two who had risen to join the battle. The trio sprawled awkwardly amid a welter of table and chairs. Without waiting for them to recover, the Penetrator vaulted the low dividing rail and headed past the startled, fearful girl.

"I think I'll check that out for myself, sweetheart," he said as he disappeared down a corridor to the executive wing.

A quick look in the offices told the Penetrator that the girl had spoken the truth. None of the big shots were present. He started back, listening to the approach of oversized shoes slapping the tile. As he turned a corner he came face to face with the three heavies.

"There he is, Dole," one cried out.

All three men filled the corridor from wall to wall with little room above them. The one in the middle, Dole, had a handful of large gun. The Penetrator had been prepared for this eventuality and, as Dole raised his piece, Mark shot him with a hissingly silent dart from Ava, his .22-caliber, CO_2-powered pistol. The sleeper round, with its neurological agent, set Dole to spasming inside of a fraction of a second. Dole's big .44 Special boomed once, a resounding blast in the confined hallway, sending a bullet harmlessly through the acoustic ceiling material, then it dropped to the floor as Dole jerked and writhed, as though bitten by a thousand ants, following it an instant later. Both the others looked on open-mouthed for a second longer, then turned to make a try at escape.

Ava hissed twice more and the unlucky pair writhed alongside Dole. The Penetrator stepped over their prostrate forms and walked back to the reception area. He fished in his coat pocket and came up with another blue flint arrowhead. He tossed it lightly on the desk in front of the wide-eyed girl.

"Here you are, sweetheart, a little souvenir to show your bosses," Mark growled from the corner of his mouth, still playing the tough-guy role to the hilt. "And . . . tell them I'll be back. That's a promise."

Dr. Raymond Barr leaned forward in the comfortable chair, which he had placed near the large living-room window of the cottage. He lifted a glass and drained half its contents. With a satisfying smack of his lips, he reached out for a wicker-covered bottle and refilled the tumbler with a crystal-white stream. He'd found a type of rum that drank like water and kicked like a Percheron. Most satisfactory.

"Come here, my dear," he instructed.

A barely nubile child from the Scum of the Earth commune swayed pigeon-toed across the living-room, sunset light glowing off her smoothly tanned, naked skin. She knelt between Dr. Barr's bare, outstretched legs and prepared to attend to his raging need. At the moment of contact, he leaned back in the chair with a sigh of contentment. His pleasure came from more than sexual gratification. The project was going well.

The lab had been in operation for two weeks now, with every indication they were on the right path. Dr. Barr's unusual schedule had disconcerted his assistants at first; twelve- to sixteen-hour shifts in the lab, alternating with a two-day absence after the first eight days. This past week they had grown accustomed. They adjusted their work loads to match the erratic habits of their superior. They had plenty of work to do, maintaining the on-going experiments, while Dr. Barr spent time away from the facility. As the daily routine smoothed out, Dr. Barr found himself with other reasons to be highly pleased.

Brad Lessor had located a seemingly inexhaustible supply of blood and bone marrow. The scientist didn't bother to inquire into the source, but felt sure that the local population might have provided the unwitting donors. During the first of his absences, at an orgiastic session of gorging on fresh seafood, liquor, drugs, and sex, Lessor had confided to Dr. Barr a great deal more about his plans for the future.

Lessor, too, had a strong dislike of blacks, held them in contempt. His feelings, however, weren't born of the same reasons that motivated Dr. Barr and his backer, Armbrewster—whose hatred seemed to grow daily, to transfer itself from those who had harmed them directly to any black man, to *all* blacks. Lessor developed his prejudice from close proximity to blacks in jails and prison. Before that he'd shared barracks space with them in the army. It was during this time, or so he told Dr. Barr, that he developed his idea of domination. That his assumptions for the future were based on a false premise didn't seem to deter him in the least. Dr. Barr, however, saw it differently.

Despite his growing prejudice, Dr. Raymond Barr still realized how effective a foe in his plans blacks could be. Because of that he dismissed the concept of a total-effort race war and felt that Lessor dreamed the dreams of the mad. The insistent burr of a telephone bell shattered Dr. Barr's reflections and his surging drive toward orgasm.

"Yes? What is it!" he snapped into the mouthpiece.

"Bowen, sir. Can you possibly come to the lab? It's extremely important, sir. I . . . I think you should see what has happened immediately."

"All right," Barr said testily. "I'll be there in ten minutes." He'd have to dress, he thought as he hung up the handset. And do something about the liquor fumes that undoubtedly issued from his mouth. He slipped into a pair of walking shorts, sandals, and a pullover knit shirt. Stopping beside the big-eyed little girl, he patted the child on her head.

"When I return, my little dove, we'll pick up where we left off, eh?"

A sharp, tingling spray of Binaca had banished the rum odor from Dr. Barr's breath by the time he reached the lab. The staff stood around, wearing expressions of excitement and anticipation. Bowen, the senior assistant, stepped forward. Before he could make any comment, Barr interrogated waspishly.

"Precisely what was so important as to drag me away from one of my few hours of rest?"

"Perhaps I should start at the beginning," Bowen stammered out.

"A logical place to begin, I would say." Dr. Barr had no intention of relenting on this violation of his rules.

"You recall that one of the routine test series you set up for us to conduct involved low level irradiation of blood samples in the presence of various chemicals? Well, we began those day before yesterday. The substance introduced into sample three-nineteen was a chemically synthesized Beta Globulin . . . a blood protein. This, in turn, was introduced into thirty blood culture dishes.

"Just before I called you we completed examination of those cultures. In every instance, *every one*, the Beta Globulin had destroyed the red blood cells in incredible quantity and at an enormously accelerated rate."

"Is this synthesized protein radioactive?" Raymond Barr thought fast, seeking a reason for his question. "I mean, could it be used as a tracer for the early detection of SCA?"

"No, sir. It's wildly globulicidal. It destroys red blood cells at a rate heretofore unknown."

"What, exactly, was done to the sample?"

"Following your instructions we exposed the Beta Globulin to the infrared chamber and the ultraviolet, with only enough gamma radiation to simulate conditions at extremely high altitudes. That was based on your theory that it might not be the lesser oxygen supply at high altitudes, but the higher incidence of exposure to radiation that causes the stimulation of the SCA syndrome."

"Yes . . . yes, go on."

"Apparently the irradiation induced a change in the nature of the Beta Globulin. It's unstable to begin with, and this sent it over into a state where the hemolysis results in leaving a thin sickle-shaped remnant of the red blood cells it attacks."

"Does it affect . . . *all* blood?"

"As per your instructions, every staff member provided blood for control samples."

"And?"

"No indication of hemolysis in any of the control samples."

Dr. Barr felt jubilant, euphoric. This might . . . *might* be it. Quickly he issued orders for additional batteries of tests, under the strictest of supervision. What he wanted, what he most needed, was a live specimen on which to test the globulicidal Beta Globulin. Perhaps Lessor could help him out there. Completing his orders to the staff, Raymond Barr hurried from the laboratory.

"Brad," Dr. Barr began when he reached the Scum of the Earth commune. "I have a special order for you to fill."

"Ask away, Doc. Whatever your heart desires."

"I need some live specimens to conduct certain tests with. Can you get me any? Perhaps some black beach bums. Or some of those street urchins . . . God knows there's plenty of them roving San Juan. They'll have to be . . . someone who won't be missed."

Lessor grinned wolfishly. "Consider it done, Doc. I'll let you know when I get it set up."

Chapter 6

FINAL TEST

Early the next morning an agitated and exhilarated Dr. Raymond Barr got on the specially installed telephone line to Joseph T. Armbrewster. He could hardly contain the joy that rang in his words.

"Is this line safe? Are you sure?" Barr questioned first.

"Of course it is. The line's like any other one, it's the telephones that are different," Armbrewster replied, grouchy at being awakened before his customary seven o'clock.

"We've got it! I think we've got the answer."

Stunned, but hopeful, Armbrewster forgot all about the disruption of his routine. "Are you sure?"

"No. Not one hundred percent. But . . . we have an unstable protein that has turned globulicidal. It eats red blood cells. Carves them out in the nicest sickle shape you've ever seen."

"What does this mean in terms of our, ah, goals?"

"That depends on my final tests. But, Joe, what it eventually means, if it works, is that we have the niggers by the balls."

"My, my, such crudity," Armbrewster said through laughter.

"Blame it on the people I have to associate with. Right now I'm so euphoric I don't care what I'm saying. Think of it. Bates, Leroy Jackson, Petty, and that animal who destroyed your daughter . . . all of them are at our mercy now."

"Yes. Them and all those who escape just punishment." Armbrewster's words were a caress, a tribute of gratitude to the efforts of the scientific team his money had bought.

"Why stop there?"

"What do you mean?"

"Look, you're living up there in, excuse me for saying so, but in your ivory tower. For nearly a month now, I've been living among *them.* I see them, smell them, have to rub elbows with them nearly every day. They've turned this beautiful island into one gigantic slum. If we . . . if we can selectively eliminate, undetected, certain undesirables—and if it proves out, that's exactly what Beta Globulin X can do—why not take it all the way? Get rid of them all."

Joe Armbrewster had never considered this aspect as a part of his revenge before. The idea was overwhelming. Perhaps the blows to his head had affected Raymond Barr more than the doctors suspected. It was madness. It was . . . genocide. He fumbled for words, aware of a long silence from the other end of the line.

"Ah . . . well, I hadn't given that idea much thought. It's something, all right. We'll . . . we'll have to give it due consideration and get back to it after the tests prove out. What say?"

"Fine. Fine." Dr. Barr's mind had already been

distracted, off on a new line of thought connected to the development of Beta Globulin X. Having vented his suppressed, but growing, hatred, he no longer addressed his mind to the issue. "I'll keep you posted."

In Gulfport, the Penetrator completed preparations for his final move against the Bayside Fisheries conglomerate. Into one of a pair of matched, lightweight metal suitcases he packed the weapons and equipment he felt he would need.

Nothing noisy or excessively destructive. So far the hired muscle for Bayside had only burnt a couple of boats and roughed up some people. This had to be a low-key operation, designed to scare the power behind Bayside with what could happen, rather than to foment open combat and leave only the bleeding pieces for the law. As he made ready to leave his motel room, the phone rang.

"Good morning, my boy. I trust you have that funny machine attached to the telephone," Professor Willard Haskins said cheerfully.

It reached the Penetrator's ears as a series of squawks and titters that bore no resemblance to human speech. That told him to attach his scrambler to the handset. "Hello, Professor. What's the occasion?"

"Some rather disturbing news from Puerto Rico. Seems some people down there think there's a plague of vampires infesting the island. There have been a number of bodies found, drained of all their blood. Thought it might be of interest to you since some of the corpses have been discovered on or near land belonging to a certain gentleman you've had particular interest in over the past few weeks."

"Joseph T. Armbrewster."

"One and the same. I don't know what or if it has any bearing on the matter you're currently involved in. But, since the same name cropped up, I felt you would want to know."

"Certainly. Thank you for filling me in. I'm about to terminate the situation here and, as soon as I do, I'll look into this other thing."

"Might I suggest you begin in Indianapolis?"

"Thinking of killing the same bird with two stones?"

Professor Haskins chuckled at the mixed metaphore. "Always trying to get one over on me. Pursue this however you think best and, meantime, I'll try to get you a contact in Indianapolis. As I recall, I have several former students who hail from there. Might be one of them could do you some good."

"All right, Professor. I'll check in when the job here is finished."

Back to Plan A, the Penetrator thought, as he carefully checked to see that his room door was securely locked. He'd hit the shipyard first, take out any of the imported goon squad that hadn't departed as ordered. A few thermite bombs, some white phosphorous, would do costly enough damage to encourage Armbrewster to shorten his horns.

In Dr. Barr's lab, a muted frenzy of activity centered on every workbench. Staff members hurried back and forth with various specimens and Dr. Barr himself manned a large, powerful binocular microscope. The twin fields of the optical device glowed with a ruddy, orange-red light each time the short, slender doctor moved his head to make a note on his case sheet. What he observed, on slide after slide, heightened his assurance that they were on the way to absolute success. At noon, he stopped work, clapping his hands to call attention to his words.

"Well, now, ladies and gentlemen. It's time for a bite to eat. There's lobster salad, boiled shrimp, champagne, and all the trimmings waiting at my cottage. After lunch we begin the most important part of our endeavor."

That afternoon's efforts to convert the Beta Globulin X into an aerosol spray wore on into the night and well into the next day before consistent results were achieved. By then the two quarts of dimethyl sulfoxide that Dr. Barr had ordered from Armbrewster had arrived by air freight. The super-lubricant, the fantastic penetration properties of which had remained unappreciated until the mid-sixties, came as a by-product of pulp paper manufacture. Once a waste substance, it now sold at close to a thousand dollars a quart.

The reason for its presence there was known only to Armbrewster and Barr. They planned to place the Beta Globulin X in suspension in DMSO, then make an aerosol spray of it so that the globulicidal protein could be absorbed into the body through contact with skin, as well as ingested by mouth or inhaled. A quick, neat way to a grisly death.

Once this compound had been mixed in a test sample, the staff began working with it on specimens of black blood and bone marrow. As they progressed, Dr. Barr strolled over to the Scum of the Earth commune to see Brad Lessor.

"Good news, Doc," Lessor greeted him. "I've found just the right guys you need. I've set it up for a meet on the beach tonight."

Being a Sunday, the Penetrator figured few, if any, sheep might be in the way at Baymaster Shipyard. He put the front gate guard to sleep with a dart from Ava and blitzed the place like a Luftwaffe strike out of the sun. Stacks of steel hull plate provided sizzling fuel for the chemical fires he ignited with his thermite grenades. The chandler's shop turned to a charcoal kiln from the blast of one WP egg. Mark worked his way quickly through the ways, igniting the thick support beams that cradled fragile ships' hulls, then down along a narrow dock.

Five members of the goon squad had not heeded the warning to leave town. They were forted up aboard a large trawler in for minor repairs. They saw the lone figure darting down the planks toward their gangway and made ready to give him a nasty greeting. One of the quintet had a submachine gun, an efficient 9mm Ingram.

The Penetrator became aware that the hoods were better armed than he when a staccato burst from the Ingram chewed slivers out of the dock planks, inches from his legs. He dived for cover behind the thick iron counterweight of a mobile crane and dug into his bag of deadly tricks.

He drew out the most devastating weapon he had brought along, an Autoburgler, the commercial name of a single-shot, 12-gauge shotgun cut down to pistol size. A few dozen ricocheting buckshot pellets would keep heads down, but hardly inflict the sort of damage he needed to create. Thinking quickly, the Penetrator loosed off a round and leaped for the crane cab.

While starting up the engine, Mark reloaded and blasted a second charge of shot out through the open right window. As the idling motor warmed up, he put in a third shell and fired again, then started the high arm with its suspended ball and hook into motion. The machine gunner popped up briefly to spray the metal monster with a short burst, effecting little damage. Bullets whined and screamed around the Penetrator, who crouched in the cab, straining his neck to see and judge his position.

When he felt the boom had reached the proper point, Mark cut in the main cable clutch and the heavy iron hook plunged downward in a rush. In the last instant the man behind the Ingram looked up. His bellow of fear cut off in a meaty, liquid-sound-ing smack, followed by a metallic clang as the hook hit the deck. The cable, impelled now by only its own momentum, played out slackly. From the opposite side of the cabin, startled yelps and heavy splashes announced the departure of two of Armbrewster's gunsels. Jumping from the crane cab, the Penetrator fired a final blast from the Autoburgler and rushed the gangplank.

He met with no resistance from the remaining pair of hoods. One was busy being sick beside the pulped red smear that had been the Ingram shooter, while the other stood, looking green and ready to vomit up his own breakfast, hands meekly held in the air. The Penetrator disarmed him and secured both gunmen with plastic riot handcuffs, leaving them and the automatic weapon of questionable origin for the police. He hurried for the main gate.

Mark skidded to a stop beside the slumbering guard. Reaching into the booth he dialed Junior Jones's number at the warehouse, gambling the hard-working fisherman would be there. The chance paid off.

"Junior? Don't ask questions, just listen. There's going to be some loud noises coming from the Bayside Fisheries offices in a few minutes. I can sure use no interruptions for awhile. Can you put in the word with the local law to keep off my back for awhile?"

"Can do . . . and . . . thanks, buddy."

Five minutes later the Penetrator kicked open the front door of Bayside Fisheries, Inc., the black hole in the muzzle of his silenced High Standard .22 tracking onto four startled faces, which looked at him in total consternation.

"Who the hell are you?" one man demanded.

"The moving man. I'm going to pack you up and kick you out of this part of the country. Go back to Armbrewster and tell him his little plan got shot full of holes."

Ted Jennings, who had spoken before, stepped forward defiantly. "Whoever you are, we have the law on our side. This is a legitimate business enterprise and you are nothing but a common criminal. A thug hired by a few malcontents."

"Cut the sermon, Jack. You're about as legitimate as the Peking government. Now, as I was saying before you so rudely interrupted me, I came here with an offer you'd be crazy to refuse. Either you tell your boss his plans got shot full of holes . . . or you four *will* be."

Jennings's eyes followed the slight movement as the fat muzzle of the seven-and-a-quarter-inch full-barrel silencer sagged almost carelessly down from his face. The weapon chuffed quietly and a forty-grain hollowpoint pellet bit into his right biceps. With a conscious effort, he compelled his body to overcome the pain and immediate numbness he felt as the little slug entered and expanded in his flesh.

"You must be out of your mind if you think that little peashooter scares us."

The guy had to be crazy to say that, the Penetrator thought. Gutsy, but nuts. He put on his grimmest snarl. "You're Jennings, no doubt. Who else would be this stupid and loud-mouthed? It's bullet placement that counts, sonny boy. The next one goes right between your beady little eyes." The muzzle rose until it became a black period that filled Jennings's entire field of vision. He paled visibly.

"Now, if you gentlemen feel more in a mood to cooperate, everyone on the floor, face down and spread-eagled."

As the terrified executives hurried to comply, Mark Hardin knelt beside each one and trussed him securely with a thin strip of serrated plastic. The riot cuffs would hold them long enough. Then he went through the offices, trashing everything not of importance and leaving revealed notations and correspondence that might prove incriminating when the police found it. At the door he tossed an arrowhead down where Jennings could see it, and walked out, leaving the hall entrance gaping.

Dr. Raymond Barr bubbled over with enthusiasm when he went to meet Brad Lessor that night. His precious compound, which he now called *Terminus,* was odorless, tasteless, and colorless. Best of all, it had absorbed through a semi-permeable membrane—a substance much like skin—and appeared to be working on the blood sample beyond, according to early microscopic examination. He struggled to contain his glee when he came upon Lessor and three youths.

"Here they are, Doc," Lessor indicated the young blacks, ranging in age from thirteen to seventeen. They wore shabby clothes and had surly, discontented mouths below hate-filled eyes. Examining them, Barr felt they hardly even represented the best of a sorry lot.

"What you got laid on, man?" the oldest of the trio asked in broken English. "You got the hots for little boys?"

"Watch your mouth, you gibbering ape!" Dr. Barr snarled back. Then composing himself, he went on in his atrocious Spanish. "How would you three like to be set up as dealers?" Lessor had already informed him that the beach bums he had rounded up were into drugs; they'd know what he meant.

"Here, man? What for? The place is lousy with it, and the price is way too low."

"No. I was thinking of . . . New York."

Mention of the magic land in the north changed their attitudes appreciably. The three dark faces still echoed suspicion and disbelief, but the eyes registered a flame of hope. "You jivin' us, whitey?"

"I'm serious. I'm thinking of setting up a little operation and I need dealers I can trust. Brad here says you're the ones.

"You've heard of the crazy doctor with a lab set up way out here?" he asked, changing tack. "Well, that's me. That lab is a heroin refinery. It'll be a closed circuit. We'll be processing our own product and distributing it. That means greater profits for you and for me. What do you say to that?"

"I still think it's a lot of honkey shit," the biggest youth replied in a growl.

"You speak pretty good English for a baboon," Barr snapped. "Now listen good. You're either in this thing or not. All the way out. It's too important an operation to have loose mouths running all over San Juan. They'll never find your bodies. *Do you dig on that, you stupid coon*?"

"*¿Que dise*?" the youngest inquired.

Quickly the middle boy filled in the younger. Eyes wide they waited fatefully for their leader's decision. Suddenly the tension ebbed from the oldest black, a weak grin spreading on his face.

"Hey, I was only jivin' a little, man. You hear me?"

"So you're in. Let's go over to the lab. You'll stay there until we can arrange new identities, clothes, all of that, and get you on a plane to Kennedy International."

Chapter 7

CONVENTIONS CAN BE HARMFUL TO YOUR HEALTH

The Penetrator aimed the nose of his Mooney 201 into the clear sky, pointing the spinner for the distant horizon. When he reached altitude he centered the needles on his nav. radios, set his heading on 010, punched the information into the flight director, and, switching on the auto-pilot, leaned back to enjoy the ride.

Two hours later, Mark took back control of the bird and began letting down into Nashville, Tennessee. He'd refuel—top off the tanks actually—grab a bite to eat, and head on to Indianapolis. Better check in with the Stronghold, he added to his mental list. He glanced at his chart, contacted the tower on the indicated frequency, and took a place in the pattern, waiting his turn to land.

"Glad you called, my boy," Professor Haskins enthused when he answered the ring. Cautious, since they were using an unsecured line, he went on. "I gather you are heading north."

"That's right. Should be there in another two, three hours."

"While you're there I suggest you look up an old student and dear friend of mine. Jim Nero. Detective Captain Jim Nero he is now."

A cop? For a moment a chill of apprehension washed over the Penetrator. Despite his long battle against crime, he and the law didn't get along all that well. How could he be sure about even an honest cop? The rewards offered, the publicity and notoriety attached to being the man who brought in the Penetrator . . . even the contract money offered by organized crime, all were powerful inducements to put in the way of underpaid and overworked lawmen. Mark's words, then, partly expressed his attitude.

"That's lovely, just wonderful. What am I supposed to do? I just walk into headquarters and say, 'Hi, I'm here to kick ass on one of your most prominent citizens.' "

"Don't be flip. Jim and I go back a long way. I was a young professor, first year to have a chair, and he was in one of my lower division GE courses. He had a natural flare for geology, but his major was police science. I spent a lot of time and many a beer at a convenient pub trying to proselytize him. It never worked. So, geology's loss became law enforcement's gain. He left the Coast about four years ago to head up the detective division back there. At least he can get you an *entrée* to that gentleman of your current interest. Give him my best."

It had been a brief and unsatisfactory phone call.

"Hi, Doc," Brad Lessor greeted Dr. Barr as the latter made ready to leave his cottage for the laboratory. "I thought you might be interested in this."

"The *local* papers? Whatever is going on around here important enough for me to labor through a Spanish language newspaper?"

"Read . . . read. It's in English."

Dr. Barr began skimming the front page of the *San Juan Star,* the leading English language newspaper in Puerto Rico. There was, he discovered, to be a large convention in San Juan. Men from all over the United States would attend. Black professional men . . . *black*! A wintery smile creased Dr. Barr's lips. He made some quick calculations. Yes . . . why not? They could rig up something. It would be the ideal field test of *Terminus.* He beamed appreciation as he turned to Lessor.

"Most perceptive, my friend Lessor. I thank you for bringing this to my attention. I think we should take a close look at our young friends this morning, and then do some careful planning. Come along, if you like."

On the previous evening, Dr. Barr had taken the three young Puerto Ricans to the lab. There he had ordered them to take a bath and, upon leaving the shower, sprayed each of them with a small quantity of *Terminus.* They had then been given places to sleep and a small supply of marijuana. Now the doctor was interested in seeing if any primary or secondary effects of the destructive protein could be detected. He hurried on up the walk and entered the building with Lessor at his side.

"Ah, yes. My enterprising young businessmen," he greeted the sullen trio. "You don't seem properly cheerful today. What's the problem?"

"You sure this crap is for makin' junk, man?" the eldest, Ramon, demanded.

"No, Ramon. Not all of it. The ether precipitation plant hasn't been brought in as yet. This is . . . ah, cover in the event of government interest in what I'm doing."

"Smart. You got it all figured out," Ramon admitted reluctantly.

"How are you feeling this morning?" Dr. Barr addressed them, his eyes keen with interest.

Lupe, the youngest, frowned. His words, in Spanish, came slowly. "That grass you gave us must have been bad. We all got headaches this morning something fierce."

"My, my. That is too bad. But, come, let me examine you. I am a doctor, you know."

Grudgingly the boys followed Dr. Barr to the rear of the laboratory. There he took blood samples, gave them each two Darvon capsules, and suggested they relax awhile in the yard behind the building. Then he sat at a small desk, doodling idly while he thought. At last he looked up and called Lessor to him.

"This is something that can't be trusted to my assistants. Once they realize what it is we're doing, they'd go to the authorities. Can we get some volunteers from your commune?"

"No sweat, Doc. You got 'em."

"Fine. Their first job will be to dispose of my assistants." Having arranged the murder of three human beings in so casual a manner, Dr. Barr turned to the main issue. "This convention constitutes the finest possible field test for *Terminus*. What we need is a means of introducing it into the air-conditioning system at the convention hotel."

"Easy again, Doc. The inlet for that sort of equipment is usually on the roof. All we need to do is take along that pressurized cylinder of yours and let is spray into the intake, got me? We can bypass the filters, so no sweat."

"Brilliant. You make it sound as though all our problems are solved in advance. Now, let me take a look at those blood samples."

Ten minutes later, with an air of extreme satisfaction, Dr. Barr leaned back from the microscope. "Perfect. Already the leukocyte count is way up. Some of the red cells show characteristic sickle-shaped residue. And their count is way below normal. Of course, it could be accounted for by malnutrition and drug abuse, so we'll have to wait another twelve hours to be sure."

"About this other thing, then? The field test?"

"Preparations will consume considerable time. We will assume that it will work as predicted and start making ready now."

"Gotcha, Doc."

The Penetrator made his first contact with Captain Nero in a restaurant two blocks from the Central Detective Bureau. They both experienced that slight, formal stiffness of two strangers meeting for the first time. Then they began to relax over coffee.

"How is old Willard?" Jim Nero asked. "I haven't seen him in years. You can imagine my surprise when he called me up the other night."

"He's an irascible as ever," Mark Hardin replied. "Did he . . . go into any details about what I'm interested in?"

"Not a great deal. Only that you . . . and he had some interest in Joe Armbrewster. Are you digging up dirt?"

"Not exactly. Is there some to shovel through?"

"Depends on how you look at it. Armbrewster is one of our lost cases."

"I don't follow you."

"It happened some years ago, before I came to Indianapolis. His daughter got . . . involved with drugs. She died of an OD. She was only fifteen. There was a young black man involved. A high-school dropout who provided her with her drugs. As it went down there was no way of obtaining proof of anything. But Armbrewster seemed obsessed with the case. He kept putting pressure on through the mayor and the City council. It became one of the first cases I handled here.

"Again, no results." Jim Nero rolled his palms upward in a negative gesture. "Oh, I worked it hard enough, but the pusher had slipped out of sight and no one was doing any talking. If you can imagine it, a black cop, especially one with rank, is resented in the black community even more than a white officer. So I got nowhere. I felt like I was shoveling shit against the tide."

Mark smiled ruefully, remembering his experiences in Saigon. "I've been there. Ah . . . tell me, could this situation have affected his business ability in any way?"

"How do you mean?"

"Could he have directed his parental affection . . . emotions that were thwarted by his daughter's death . . . into his business? In other words, might he have sublimated his bitterness and grief into a drive for greater wealth and power, no matter how or by what means he obtained them?"

"*Hmmm.* I have heard some whispers about Armbrewster Steel and some of the dealings involving old Joe. But, nothing definite. It'll take me a couple of days to dig up something tangible. That okay?"

"Fine with me," the Penetrator replied.

"Business ethics . . . empire building . . ." Jim Nero speculated aloud. "Are you with the government? The feds?"

The Penetrator looked blank, but tried for sincerity. "I'm just a friend of Willard Haskins. Call this an interest in a company we might want to invest in."

"Oh, sure. Sure. I'll try to remember that. Where do I contact you?"

"I'll call you at your office day after tomorrow."

A chill, moist wind off the sea brushed over Dr. Raymond Barr and three members of the Scum of the Earth as they lay crouched on the rooftop of the Hotel San Juan. Occasional spatters of rain fell from the clouds that obscured the sky, threatening a real downpour. Even without the overhead murk, this was an ideal night, in the dark of the moon. They huddled near the wheezing, clanking, old-fashioned, air-conditioning system, working as quietly as possible.

"We're ready, Doc," Brad Lessor whispered.

"Fine," Dr. Barr replied, releasing the valve on his aerosol cylinder. "Here it comes." His mind filled in the hissing he could not actually hear as the deadly Beta Globulin X spewed out into the ventilating system. A beatific smile spread over his face.

Below the hovering forms on the roof, in the banquet room, over a hundred of the nation's most notable citizens of African origin were talking politely over the conch steaks flown in specially from Nassau. Their pleasure was somewhat restrained, saving their appreciation for the next course of prime rib. Among the conventioneers sat doctors, lawyers, clergymen, and entertainers. Half a dozen well-known sports figures graced the head table. The men and their wives were being feted in the best style the island could provide. They were looking forward to the address by Dr. Alfonso de Vega, outspoken head of the Puerto Rican independence movement. Everyone present was unaware that Death had become the master of ceremonies.

"So, my mysterious new friend, we meet at the appointed hour."

"I thought your major was police science, not theater . . . bad theater," the Penetrator quipped as he shook hands with Captain Jim Nero. The policeman laughed hugely.

"This is all sort of irregular, you know. I couldn't resist the opportunity to make a drama of it. Now, as to what I've found. In a word, nothing. Or at least, damn little. Armbrewster is successful, ambitious, and, so far as anyone around here knows, entirely aboveboard. The only thing that seems out of the normal routine is so insignificant I hesitate to tell you."

"Tell me anyway."

Nero sipped at his before-lunch Old-Fashioned. "Until two mongths ago, Armbrewster has had several properties up for sale. He's seemed quite anxious to rid himself of them. Then, right in the middle of negotiations for one particular bit of acreage, he took them all off the market."

"Those real estate parcels don't happen to be along the Gulf Coast, by any chance?"

"No. They're in Puerto Rico."

"Puerto Rico?" The penetrator began out loud, then lapsed into thought. What did that have to do with the Bayside conglomerate? And where had he heard about a connection between Armbrewster and Puerto Rico? Then he had it. The supposed vampire victims. Some of the bodies had been found on or near property belonging to Armbrewster. Mark decided to try his new source for any possible insight that might tie Armbrewster to the killings.

"This might sound like an off-the-wall question, but, believe me, it may have something to do with Armbrewster. Recently I heard about some corpses found in Puerto Rico. Several of them were on property that belonged to Armbrewster. They'd been drained of their blood and someone down there let the press get ahold of a suspicion that a vampire might be involved. I don't suppose you believe in vampires any more than I do. What I'd like to know is, were any of the victims blacks?"

"That shouldn't take too long to find out." Jim

Nero left the table, heading for a pay phone in a secluded alcove off the cashier's desk. While he was gone, their food arrived. Mark sat patiently awaiting the return of the black detective.

When Captain Nero approached the table, his face was clinched down into a frowning scowl. Obviously something had come up to deeply disturb him. "Well, what's the word?" the Penetrator asked.

"All of them. They were all black."

"Any indication that Armbrewster might be implicated in their deaths?"

"You mean . . . because of that thing with his daughter?" At Mark's affirmative nod, he went on. "No. Armbrewster hasn't been in Puerto Rico for seven years. Just a coincidence, nothing more."

If this news wasn't the cause of the black detective's depressed state and obvious worry, what could be? The Penetrator decided to ask.

"Did you see the news this morning?" Jim Nero said in reply. "About . . . about all of those black people dying suddenly and inexplicably from sickle cell anemia? It's . . . my God. it's horrible. Oh," he raised a deprecating hand. "I'm not going to play pity the poor, afflicted black with you. SCA is a fact of life that every black man and woman must learn to live with. It's . . . like any other genetic disease. The Jews have Tay-Sachs and we've got SCA. And we can get everything you honkeys can come down with, too." His smile took the sting out of the racial epithet.

"What makes this so horrible," he went on, "is that all of a sudden, all over the nation, people are dying of it. Like within hours of each other. Prominent people, I mean. And not just them, alone. Their wives or husbands, even some children."

Something else from the recent news was trying to wriggle itself to the surface of the Penetrator's brain. An echo of thought came through, but not enough.

"All right. Cool down and put that mind of yours to work. You didn't seem all that agitated about it before making the phone call. Tell me, what else do these people have in common besides being prominent and black? Something you may have heard, but that didn't register until now."

Captain Nero thought for a moment. "Well, now . . . *hmmm* . . . it did say on the news that some of them had just returned from a convention of outstanding Afro-American professional persons."

"Some of them?" Mark interrupted. "Could it have been that all of them were at the convention?" The Penetrator leaned forward with the eager realization he had hit on something.

Captain Nero brightened. "It's worth a fifty-dollar bet they did."

"Where was that convention held?"

"In . . . Puerto Rico!"

"For the time being, I rest my case. Right now, I'd like very much to know where Mr. Joseph T. Armbrewster happens to be." He'd also like to know, Mark thought, how the hell this tied into the Gulf Coast fishing industry.

Their meal forgotten, both men huddled around the telephone. Captain Nero took the receiver, feeding coins into the slot. He dialed a number and waited. When the receptionist at Armbrewster Steel came on the line he spoke carefully and distinctly.

"This is Captain James Nero, Central Detective Division, IPD. I'd like to speak to Mr. Joseph Armbrewster."

"I'm sorry, sir, he's not here today."

"Do you know where he might be reached?"

"I can't help you there, perhaps his secretary knows. I'll transfer you."

The secretary came on the line and Captain Nero went through the identification routine again. After a slight pause, the woman at the other end came back with a warmer, more relaxed voice. "Oh, yes, Captain. I remember you now. Is it . . . something about Stacey? Something Mr. Armbrewster would want to know?"

"Yes. Perhaps. I'm sorry, but I can't discuss it with anyone but Mr. Armbrewster. How might I reach him?"

"I'm not really sure you can. He's left the city."

"For where?"

"San Juan."

"Puerto Rico?"

"That's correct, sir."

"Thank you." Captain Nero hung up the handset. "He's gone. Heading for . . ."

"Small coincidences, eh? I'm most grateful, Captain. I owe you a steak, next time I'm in Indianapolis. Thanks so very much."

"Wait! What do you mean next time you're in town? Where are you going?"

"Puerto Rico . . . where else?"

"Hold on there. Dammit, wait for me!"

The Penetrator left Detective Captain Jim Nero standing in the restaurant lobby, waving a hand helplessly at his departing back.

Chapter 8

UNFORTUNATE ARRIVAL

Joseph T. Armbrewster seethed with fury. As much at the helplessness of his anger over an irreversible event as at the perpetrator of it.

Seated across from him in the suite at the *Nacional de San Juan,* Dr. Raymond Barr bubbled with excitement and satisfaction he found hard to contain. Neither man spoke for several minutes.

"You idiot!" Armbrewster thundered. "You stupid son-of-a-bitch! You know we were to keep this secret, not to let anything slip. That it was to be for use on certain individuals we'd agreed upon in advance. Why? Why in the hell did you go ahead with this insane scheme without at least consulting me?"

"But it worked," Dr. Barr burbled, enraptured at his own success. "They're dying like flies. And we did discuss it, you know. Remember my saying to you that there was no reason to limit our goal to a few paltry criminals. That we had a chance with

Terminus to rid this otherwise beautiful nation of the African menace before it overwhelms us. Besides," he added defensively. "I needed a definitive field test to determine if it would work as we wanted, when and where we wanted and under any conditions. The results were spectacular, the success enormous."

"Christ! It got enormous attention from the press, too."

"So what? Let the vermin shake in their shoes, wondering where and when it will strike again." Dr. Barr's eyes glittered with the peculiar light of madness as he sat rubbing his hands together, gloating on their deadly discovery.

"You want a gang of government investigators down here? The niggers are sacred today. Nobody is allowed to say anything against them and no one dares protect himself from them. By the time the liberal press gets through whipping this up, it'll be a greater holocaust than the Six Million. And we'll be caught right in the middle."

"I don't see that at all. Let them scream and rage, let them investigate. How can they possibly trace it back to us? Why, there's nothing been said to indicate that they even know it isn't really sickle cell anemia."

"It isn't?" The revelation had stunned Armbrewster out of his furor.

"Of course not. I explained all that to you. All this is is a simple unstable Beta Globulin protein that's present in everyone's blood. The only difference comes in that, after being irradiated, it becomes more unstable and in the presence of black blood becomes hemophagic, globulicidal. It eats red blood cells. It's mere coincidence that it happens to leave a sickle-cell-shaped residue. *I* don't even know why it does what it does. All I know is that it works. So, unless the researchers know exactly what it is they're looking for, I give them five years before they come up with the cause, let alone who's responsible."

Barr's words acted calmingly upon Joe Armbrewster. The steel magnate sat back, the strong fingers of one hand stroking his chin. *Terminus* did fit in with his plans. And Barr did have a point. With one blow they could wipe out the high crime rate, welfarism, race mixing, and forced integration. No! He brought himself up abruptly. He couldn't be seriously thinking like that. He was starting to sound like the nutty little scientist.

To Barr, he said, "Well, it's done with. No matter. Nothing can change that. But I don't want any more testing. Do you understand? I'll be going back to Indianapolis in the morning. When I get there, I'll start laying plans for getting the ones that *Terminus* was meant for. I'll be in touch. Be ready to pack up and head for home. Until then, do nothing, you hear, absolutely nothing more."

The Penetrator arrived in Puerto Rico at noon the next day, having island-hopped his Mooney 201 from Miami to Nassau to Santo Domingo and finally into the airport at San Juan. With a single person aboard and a light luggage load, there had been no need for this roundabout way. Only a single refueling stop would have been necessary after leaving Miami; the Mooney's range gave it over seven hundred fifty miles at seventy-five percent power and that translated to 197 miles per hour, at 18.1 mpg. But Mark had never flown over that area of the Caribbean before and he had a slight mistrust of the weather. As it happened, the passage proved uneventful.

As he taxied up to the general aviation ramp and cut the switches he had already begun to suffer from the oppressive humidity. Huge wet stains showed under each arm and he had reached over to pop open the door to aid ventilation. Climbing out, he asked the line boy to see his tanks were topped off and the plane made ready for immediate departure. He instructed the boy to also check the oil and be sure the Mooney got well tied down, as he wasn't sure how long he'd be there. That the conversation had been conducted in rapid-fire, clear Spanish insured the Penetrator the utmost in cooperation and service. Clutching a pair of metal suitcases, one filled with clothes, the other arms, he headed for the smaller general aviation terminal, sweat beads popping out on his forehead.

Outside the terminal front a rag tag collection of small boys crowded the sidewalk, spilling over into the gutter. Most were barefoot, and they wore shabby, dirt-incrusted clothes. They extended grubby hands, begging, while huge, hungry eyes looked out of gaunt, smudged faces. These were the street urchins of San Juan. Some were the illegitimate offspring of black prostitutes, others—Latinos and blacks alike—the abandoned children of families too overburdened with hungry mouths. Among them, too, were some runaways. They all shared a common berth in poverty and misery at the bottom of society. Mark Hardin shouldered his way through them, ignoring their pleas.

The Penetrator's actions weren't motivated by any lack of sympathy or callous indifference. He remembered well the lesson of the bears in the national park. Long accustomed to subsisting on handouts from tourists, when the regulations changed, the easy pickings ceased for these bears. Some of them went back to the wild, seeking berries, fish, and other naural bear foods. But others, second and third generation recipients of human largesse, simply sat down and died. They'd rather starve, it seemed, than work for a living. Welfarism had created a dependency almost impossible to break. There was a lesson in that for human relations, Mark thought, and had long steeled himself against contributing to any sort of dependency. Once free of the begging, hectoring gaggle of boys, he headed toward the taxi stand.

Mark picked the second taxi in line, from a habit trained into him during his years in Army intelligence, and asked to be taken to an inexpensive, clean motel. As the cab wheeled into traffic, a ginger-haired, gangly youth, who'd been talking with one cabby, climbed into the vehicle and gave instructions to follow.

"I tell you it's him," the acne-scarred young man reported to Brad Lessor an hour later. "It's the same fuckin' guy. I spotted him at the airport and followed him to his motel.

"So what? Take it easy, Sammy. He's no threat to us."

"Don't be so sure. I was there when he tore into Preacher Mann. He was kickin' ass and takin' names all over the place. I tell you, this Penetrator dude is bad news."

"So maybe he's here after something else . . . or takin' a vacation, for all you know."

Sammy shook his head violently. Before continuing he touched fire to a cigarette. "No way. I figure he's here because of all those black dudes dying. Your good buddy the mad scientist has stirred up more trouble than he can handle."

Brad Lessor thought for some time before coming to a decision. "Okay. Let's say you're right. This Penetrator guy is after the Doc. Well, Dr. Barr and his magic potion are the key to success for our plans to be top dogs after the fur stops flying. We can't let anything happen to him. So, if the Doc can't take care of the Penetrator himself, we're going to have to do it for him." Lessor's words brought a surprised look to Sammy's face. "The best defense is a good offense, right? That means that instead of our waiting for the Penetrator to come to us, we go after him.

"Oh, I've heard of him, know about some of the things he's done. He's dangerous, all right, but Dr. Barr has to be protected at all costs. Besides, there's all that lovely money to be had from a bunch of contracts on the Penetrator's head."

Chapter 9

PITFALLS

Leg work, routine. The curse of every police detective and the absolutely necessary heart of any investigation. Lacking any specific direction to strike, the Penetrator had been forced into this age-old, but proven method.

On the way between Indianapolis and Miami, Mark had turned up the audio portion of his ADF—the direction finder tuned to a commercial broadcast station—to get a little music. He learned from a newscast that black staff members of the Hotel San Juan were likewise dying. All attention was now focused on the convention as the single common factor, yet no specific reason could be given for the rising death toll. The Penetrator made the Hotel San Juan his first stop.

"I am sorry, *señor*," the barely polite desk clerk informed Mark. "We are answering no questions from the press."

"But surely you must realize that this has become a disaster of national proportions."

"No comment."

"I'd like to speak to a few of the staff."

"Absolutely not."

First try and he'd shot a blank. At the assessor's office, the Penetrator became a man interested in buying land in Puerto Rico, his reporter's guise left behind at the San Juan. Being a territory, Puerto Rican property taxes are attractively low and the officials anxious to encourage new business and residents. They laid open the books, allowing the Penetrator to determine the exact location, size, and nature of taxable structures on Armbrewster's land holdings. But this was only a first step.

In another government building, built in the Spanish Colonial style, he talked with officials of the U.S. Public Health Service. This time he used the fake Justice Department credentials provided for him long ago by Dan Griggs. That brought the most revealing answers.

"In addition to the deaths of conventioneers and the hotel staff, three more bodies have been discovered that may or may not have some bearing on this case."

"How's that?" the Penetrator inquired.

Dr. Irene Bascomb studied her visitor. "Seeing as how you're with the Justice Department, I suppose it is all right to go into detail."

"Please do."

"The bodies were of three Negro youths," the doctor began, consulting autopsy reports lying before her on the desk. "Aged thirteen, fourteen, and seventeen. Evidence of malnutrition, drug use, etc., etc. In other words they were vagabonds, street urchins, or beachcombers, persons of that nature. Here's the part that counts. Their hemoglobin count was almost zero. All that remained was a grainy residue of sickle-shaped fragments. Actual cause of death: respiratory and cardiac arrest due to oxygen starvation of the brain. That cause is consistent in every way with the convention deaths.

"But the autopsy surgeon isn't satisfied that it fits what is known of sickle cell anemia."

"What does that mean? Does he believe it might have been caused by something artificial?"

"In the light of the mass deaths resulting from exposure at the convention, that is his opinion. And mine, too."

"Were these youths at the hotel?"

"The autopsy places their time of death at some sixty hours *before* the first reported convention cases."

"I see. Where were they found?"

"The bodies were located in shallow, hastily dug graves along a country road." Dr. Bascomb reached into a desk drawer for a map of Puerto Rico. "Right along . . . here."

The Penetrator bent forward to examine the locale indicated by the doctor's pointing finger. The gravesite was three miles from Armbrewster's warehouse and beach cottage. "Thank you very much, Doctor. This has been most enlightening."

Mark Hardin took his leave of the Public Health Service doctor. As he closed the door behind him and started toward the enclosed central patio, its tiled expanse crowded with tropical vegetation, his highly developed intuitive sixth sense warned him to jump backward. A huge earthenware pot, heavy with dirt and a planted palm, plummeted to the ground in the exact spot he would have occupied.

"Dammit, Benny, we missed!" Sammy griped.

"I couldn't help it, Sammy. That damned thing was heavy," the younger Scum member protested.

"We'll have to do better than that if we expect to

eliminate the Penetrator, Benny. From now on, no excuses."

"So what are we going to do now?"

"We're following him, right? Well, we're gonna keep on following him until the right opportunity presents itself."

The Penetrator drove out past the site where the three black youths had been buried, then tried every approach to the private road that led to Armbrewster's property. He refrained from going there directly. He was a stranger and would stand out from the locals in such a way that could alert whoever might be there. As far as making a soft penetration into an unknown situation, he doubted any chance existed to carry it off. He drove back to town, had a satisfying seafood dinner at a small restaurant on the waterfront, and then went to his motel for a good night's sleep.

While Mark slept, shadowy figures lurked around his rental car. Using a hard-fiber, dynamite-cap, crimping tool, Sammy squeezed each of the brake lines. Then, undetected, he and Benny slipped off into the night.

When Sammy reported to Brad Lessor, the leader made a quick decision. "He'll be coming out this way again, that's for sure. We'll just have to arrange a little surprise for him."

Early the next morning, the Penetrator started out for the area of Armbrewster's warehouse. He planned to park some distance from the exact location and move in overland. As he left the motel he noticed a seeming sluggishness to the brakes, but nothing he felt he needed to be concerned about. Half an hour later, his unconcern came back to him with a vengeance.

As Mark rounded a curve, a burro and cart suddenly bolted into the road. The Penetrator swerved and braked. Sudden, maximum pressure caused the crimped lines to give away. Brake fluid spurted from four weakened spots, quickly emptying the reservoir as Mark pumped on his brakes. He had great cause to work with such desperation, because thundering down the road toward him came a heavily loaded eighteen wheeler. . . .

Sammy Kelso and his partner Benny had waited in the brush with the burro and cart from the time the tail car had reported that the Penetrator had turned into this particular side road. They tensed as they listened to the growing sound of an approaching engine. As soon as they had positive identification, Sammy depressed the key on a walkie-talkie and spoke tersely.

"He's comin', Brad. Wind 'er up."

Then he popped the half-drowsing burro with the electrodes of a cattle prod. The animal jolted into explosive action, leaping out into the road directly in front of the oncoming car.

"We got him . . . we got the son-of-a-bitch!" Sammy yelled, as the Penetrator's car swerved and began to slow, then rushed ahead again when the sabotaged brake lines split open.

At the same moment, Brad Lessor rumbled into the other end of the curve, high-balling a stolen eighteen wheeler. He bore down on the helpless automobile. At what seemed the last possible instant, the Penetrator stopped trying to brake the car, spun the wheel in the opposite direction and floorboarded the accelerator.

Gravel spinning from the rear wheels, the Penetrator's car broke free of its deadly slide and roared past parallel to the big truck, so close that the side-view mirror was broken off. Knowing the impossibility of trying to stop, let alone reverse directions with the tractor-trailer, Lessor snarled angrily as he had to continue on. Behind the disappearing Granada, Sammy and Benny shouted and gesticulated in frustrated defeat.

The Penetrator had no doubt that someone out there had a determined intention of exterminating him. Once he was some distance from the scene of the near collision, he stopped to inspect the car. He immediately noticed the crimped brake lines. There'd been that falling urn, now this. He would have to exercise greater caution. First, he wanted to complete that close look at the Armbrewster property.

A little over an hour later, after returning the rental car and explaining about the brakes failing, Mark eased himself into the notch of a tree branch, peering through the foliage at a large cement block building. This had to be Armbrewster's warehouse. As he watched, an unknown man, about twenty-six years of age, approached, accompanied by a younger person who looked vaguely familiar to the Penetrator. He couldn't place the pimply-faced youth, though, anymore than he could successfully tell what went on inside the building from his present vantage point. The Penetrator continued his observations until nearly dark and came away no wiser than before.

"Perfect. Perfect," Dr. Raymond Barr mumbled to himself as he glanced over report after report regarding the wave of death that had overtaken the participants in the convention. The results exceeded his greatest expectations. Their ultimate weapon existed now, ready to be employed. He had to let Joe Armbrewster know, show him that not the least suspicion had been directed their way. They could safely use *Terminus* to get their revenge. His thoughts were interrupted when Brad Lessor entered the lab.

"Doc, we've got a problem here you should know about."

"What's that, Brad?"

Quickly Brad Lesson filled the scientist in on the Penetrator. He concluded by adding, "Now that you've let the lab staff go and we've taken care of your assistants, I think a couple of the guys should be with you at all times. The Penetrator is the worst kind of bad news. He was seen twice in this area, so it's crazy not to believe he's after you."

Raymond Barr sighed. "Bodyguards . . . threatened by some unknown avenger . . . they're of no consequence now, Brad. We're ready. It works as predicted, even more efficiently than I had hoped. I was just about to call Mr. Armbrewster."

"Go ahead."

Armbrewster answered on the fourth ring. The tone of his voice still indicated his displeasure with Barr's public testing of the deadly spray. He listened to what the biochemist had to say without comment, though, then made reply.

"Okay. So now we are ready to use it as it was intended to be used. The only problem is that the detectives I hired have been unable to locate any of those . . . ah, responsible for our loss."

Barr felt suddenly numb. This couldn't be happening. He couldn't have worked so hard, only to be cheated out of his revenge again. He had to ask the question he feared to have answered. "Any indication they have left Indianapolis?"

"No. They're here somewhere."

Barr's worries evaporated. "Not to worry, then." His voice became intense as he went on to explain. "It worked well enough on a hotel, it can do as well on an enire city. If they're in Indianapolis, we'll get them all right."

"The . . . the entire city? I . . . *hmmm.*" Joseph Armbrewster's mind warred against itself. For so long he had harbored a desire for vengeance, had let his desire for retribution fester inside him until it had come to influence every aspect of his life, and his business dealings. Yet, a part of him recoiled at the thought of mass murder. How could anyone seriously consider it? He wanted to dominate the blacks, make them grovel. Money, power and revenge . . . these three things guided his conscious efforts. For the past five years, his thwarted desire for the last had found at least partial solace in acquiring the other two. Even his abortive attempt to dominate the Gulf Coast fishing industry had been born of a desire to obtain his own form of revenge upon blacks, to even the score for Stacey. Dead they could no longer suffer. Alive and crushed under the heel of his power, they would spend lives of misery and degradation for what had been done. But he had to make some sort of answer to Barr.

"Just Indianapolis, eh?" he finally replied. "I mean that, Raymond. If we confine ourselves for the time being to making the guilty pay, I suppose this means might well be the only one to assure success. Okay. I'll go along on that condition. How soon can you be packed up there and leave for here?"

"I will be on a morning flight." Raymond Barr glowed with excitement. The day was at hand.

Mark Hardin decided on a stroll along the beach after his evening meal. The setting sun cast long fingers of red and purple across the glittering waters of the bay as he inhaled deeply of a salty tang that made his body tingle. He passed a few strolling couples and then came to a stretch of deserted sand. Lights of many boats winked in the harbor, and across the expanse of water loomed the shadow-cloaked ramparts of El Morro Castle. Mark breathed deeply again and turned away, back toward the bright lights of the city.

When he started up a short flight of steps that took him back to the sidewalk along the Melecon, a figure approached. The white youth, bearded and shabbily clothed, stopped before Mark. He extended a grubby hand.

"Hey, man. You got a quarter?"

Mark was about to suggest to the begging lout that if he were to get off his ass and work for a living he'd have a lot more than a quarter, when he noticed movement to both sides and behind him. Suddenly the Penetrator discovered he had become the target of a mugging.

Chapter 10

LOCKING THE BARN DOOR

Angel Dust and Hash, known as Joe Nichols and Peter Wells before joining the Scum of the Earth, couldn't understand why everyone else thought this turkey was so hard to take. Hell, he'd walked right into their little mugging scene like a blind man. As they rushed toward the Penetrator, they grinned at each other, a silent acknowledgement of how easy the hit would be. The setting sun stained their knife blades blood-red as they closed to strike.

Then their target disappeared! Instead of steel biting into yielding flesh, their shoulders thudded together as they met in the space formerly occupied by their intended victim. As they began to converge, the Penetrator had made a slight movement backward and to one side so that now he had them at the disadvantage.

Angel Dust felt an incredible pain in his right kidney. He hurt so badly he tried to cry out, but no sound would come. Jerked by his long hair, his head snapped backward as a hard fist crached into his temple. Blackness poured over him like the tide as he sank to the rough pavement. A pistol appeared in the third mugger's hand.

B.J., known as Dwayne Niel to his parents and former schoolmates before he joined the Scum, had always considered himself a hot item with a gun. He brought the muzzle into line and fired. Three bullets thudded into flesh.

But the Penetrator's hide remained unpunctured. As he finished with Angel Dust, he had turned his attentions to Hash, catching the wildly flailing youth by one wrist and propelling him forward in an arc toward B.J. Too late, Mark saw the third mugger draw his gun. The bullets took Hash high in his back, two of them bursting his heart, the third pulping a lung. Blood fountained from his lifeless lips as he crumpled into the gutter. Now the Penetrator faced only a single man. An armed and dangerous enemy.

Killing his companion momentarily shocked B.J. into motionless confusion. As he realized his predicament and the fact that their target still lived, he made another try. In that instant he stood locked in horrified surprise, though, the Penetrator had not been idle.

As B.J. swung the muzzle toward the Penetrator, he found himself looking into the single black eye of Mark's Star PD. B.J.'s lips formed a large, cartoon-character *O* around his gaping mouth, effectively eliminating an external entry wound as the 185-grain jacketed hollowpoint passed between his parted teeth and smashed upward into his brain. The PD recoiled, whipping violently to the right, but its light weight allowed the Penetrator to bring it quickly back onto target. He had no need for a second bullet.

B.J. lay on his back, stretched out in finality. A

large irregular chunk of skull, held on by a small flap of scalp, lay beyond his scraggly hair. Blood, fluid, and gray matter oozed out to stain the sidewalk. His sightless eyes bulged from their sockets and a wheeze of air expelled from his lungs as his body quivered in a palsied death tremor. From behind the Penetrator's back, a moan drew his attention.

Bending over Angel Dust, the Penetrator watched silently as the youth regained consciousness. Angel Dust's eyes slowly focused on the unwavering muzzle of the .45 in Mark's hand. The corners of his mouth twitched in barely restrained terror as he saw eternity beckoning in the black pit. Time was running out for both of them. The Penetrator grabbed Angel Dust by the shirt front and shook him, sending new spasms of pain throughout his throbbing head.

"All right, creep. Who are you and who sent you after me?"

"We . . . we're the Scum of the Earth."

"You're telling me?"

"Th-that's our family, man. The Scum of the Earth. Brad Lessor, our guru . . . he's the one sent us. Him an' the crazy Doc."

"What doctor?"

"Some looney named Barr. He's made up some sort of juice to snuff all the spades. 'Least that's what he says."

A means for killing all blacks? The pieces began to fall into place for the Penetrator. "You're doing fine. The longer you talk, the longer you live. Tell me about this doctor."

"He's crazy, I tell you. He cooked up some sort of chemical or something that takes off black people. Got this big laboratory and all, out there in the boonies. But he's nuts. Keeps talking to this chick that ain't even there, know what I mean?" Angel Dust had recovered some from his fright. He grinned lopsidedly. "But that don't keep him from diggin' on the young chickies, you know, thirteen, fourteen, fifteen . . . he goes for 'em all. Lessor kept him supplied with nookie while the Doc whipped up his brew. The old kook thinks he's in charge, but it's really Lessor. 'Least, that's what Brad tells us."

"Where's Armbrewster fit into this?"

"Armbrewster? Oh . . . him. It's his place the Doc works at. An' the old man himself came down and chewed ass after the Doc used the stuff on those spades at the convention."

Mark added this item of news to his mental file. "Is this doctor there now?"

"Maybe. When we left to set you up, he an' Lessor were getting things packed. Seems they're to get together with Armbrewster and put the stuff into use."

"Okay, turkey. You talked enough to buy yourself a free ride out of here. First, though, I need a little time to operate." As he spoke, Mark slapped Angel Dust alongside the head with the slide of his Star PD. Then he trussed up the Scum of the Earth punk, using riot handcuffs. In the distance a siren wailed, drawing nearer. Angel Dust would have enough problems in his immediate future explaining the double killing to police. He dropped an arrowhead in the unconscious man's open hand, then left hurriedly.

"Right. He's doing like you said," Brad Lessor spoke into the telephone. "He's packing his own things now. I don't know how much longer I can control him, though, Mr. Armbrewster. He's getting crazier all the time. I thought I'd crap my pants when he wanted to use it on all of Indianapolis. . . . I know you both have every reason to feel like you do. But things aren't right just yet. Look, I think what we'd better do is come along up there with him. Sort of keep an eye on him. That way, if we have to, we can snuff him and take over ourselves. You agree? . . . Okay, Mr. Armbrewster. I appreciate your trust in me, an' I'll see everything is done like you wanted. Good night."

Moving through the underbrush with only the slightest whisper of sound, the Penetrator closed in on Barr's lab in the midnight blackness. In the near distance, patches of light glowed on the ground, projected from the laboratory windows. Apparently business went on as usual. In his left hand he clutched the short, thick tube of an M-79 grenade launcher. With his right he kept small branches and vines from his face. When he reached the spot where the clearing began, some fifty yards from the building, he stopped and made ready. Keeping an eye on the only door, he called out to those inside.

"You in the laboratory. Come out peacefully and there'll be no trouble."

"Fuck you, fuzz!" a voice yelled.

"This is not the police and I'm not bound by their rules. Come out of there or I'll kill every one of you."

A shotgun blasted a reply to the Penetrator's demands, pellets slashing foliage some twenty feet to one side.

Mark's M-79 coughed sharply, lobbing a gas round in a slight arc that sent it crashing through glass. A small pop showered the inside room with CN. Despite the tear gas, the shotgun boomed twice more.

"We got gas masks, pig. That won't do you any good."

Mark loaded another of the short, stubby rounds, this one HE. Following the launching bark, glass tinkled and a loud blast filled the night. All the windows splintered outward and moans followed, as the lights flickered and went out. More shots came from the building. Mark dropped a final round into the open breech, its yellow-striped body illuminated by starlight. He let loose the white phosphorous projectile, which turned midnight to noon inside the besieged laboratory. Voices screamed in agony and two of the gunmen burst from the door, firing as they came.

Mark laid aside the M-79 and pulled his Sidewinder around into position. A pair of three-round bursts stitched across the Scum of the Earth gunmen, crumpling them into lifeless huddles on the ground. The Penetrator charged the building, bending low and firing toward the door as he ran.

As he neared the entrance a third man crashed into him. They both staggered backward, the Penetrator keeping his feet as the other fell, shrieking in pain from the glowing blobs of sticky phosphorous that burned into his flesh. The Penetrator stepped over him, the muzzle of his Sidewinder steadied on the man's chest.

"Doctor Barr? Is he inside?"

"No. No, man. Oh, God, help me. It burns so much . . ." His words broke off in a keening cry.

"Where is he?"

"Gone. All of them are gone. Lessor, too. They left us here, a trap to get you. They're gonna do in all the bloods in Indianapolis, man. You're too late to stop them." Suddenly his eyes went wide and his mouth wrenched into an agonized shape as he howled in pain and fear. One small piece of the white phosphorous had burned its way past his ribs and sent up a plume of steam as it boiled blood in his left lung. His body convulsed and throat-tearing screams came from deep in his tortured body.

It was an act of mercy, the Penetrator realized, when he shot the man, ending his agony.

Chapter 11

BACK HOME AGAIN IN INDIANA

"Indianapolis Approach Control, this is Two-Zero-One Lima Delta. I have completed descent from Nine Thousand to Five and am holding with a heading of Three-Three."

"Zero-One Lima Delta. Uh, Zero-One Lima Delta, turn right at once to Zero-Two-Zero and hold until advised. Squawk Two-Zero-One-Zero for Ident please. Be advised there is traffic at your altitude about one mile on your left and rising traffic through Five Angels on outbound vector Sierra Golf that should pass in front of you."

"Zero-One Lima Delta, Roger." The emotionless voices crackled their messages back and forth as the Penetrator's Mooney 201 was brought in to land. Once he'd cut the last switch and seen to tie-down, the Penetrator rented a car and headed for town. Thirteen hours, forty minutes from San Juan to Indianapolis, he thought as he rode along, not a bad average, all considered. Mark's mind turned to the immediate problem. There was one person he very much needed to talk to.

"So you're back, I see," Captain Jim Nero boomed heartily as Mark entered his glass-walled office.

"Sure am. And I think I've found out where Joseph Armbrewster figures into a lot of things."

"You were asking questions about his business ethics. From the look on your face, there's something a lot more important involved."

"I'm afraid there is. Remember when we were talking about sickle cell anemia? Apparently Armbrewster has financed the development of some substance that induces sickle cell anemia."

"How? That's not possible, is it? SCA's a genetic disease. It afflicts only my people. What could he possibly have in mind to do that?"

"I don't know what his motive is. But believe me when I say it is what he's done."

"Who would be crazy enough to bring about a thing like that?"

"A biochemist named Raymond Barr was mentioned in connection with this project of Armbrewster's."

"Barr! By God, he's another of my lost cases." Quickly Captain Nero filled Mark in on the history of Dr. Barr's tragedy and the results. "So it has to have something to do with their past problems. The ones at fault were all black."

"Did either show any animosity toward you? You know what I mean."

"The black cop not looking too hard for the black criminal? No. Nothing like that. In Armbrewster's case I came into it late, long after the file had been put in Pending. As to Barr, he seemed grateful to me for all I did. After all, it wasn't faulty police work that set them free, it was these goddamned liberal courts. But you've seen that before and so have I. Makes a man sick the way these mush-brained judges think more of the criminal's rights than those of his victims. Slap their wrists, pat 'em on the po-po, and send them out to sin again. Makes you wonder if they aren't doing it just to justify their own existence and make work for the whole system.

"*Awh*, hell, don't get me started on that sermon or we'll be here half the night. This isn't relevant to Barr or Armbrewster. What can we do about them?"

"They are supposed to be here in town, or somewhere in Indiana."

"I can get out an APB on them. No problem on descriptions. Anything else?"

"There's a guy named Lessor. Brad Lessor, sort of a big daddy to a cult-like hippy family that calls itself the Scum of the Earth."

"Nice name."

"Believe me, it fits. See if anything can be developed on him or them from NCIC and your records."

"Meanwhile, what will you be doing?"

"I'm going to have a little look around of my own."

"Good luck."

"Good evening from Chicago. Tonight, ABC News begins a Special Report on sickle cell anemia. This once rare, but heartbreakingly incurable, genetic disease has begun to decimate the black population of America at an alarming rate." The familiar features of ABC's black anchorman in Chicago glowed on the screen, his features appropriately grim for the message he delivered. "You recall that a week ago, the nation was rocked by the sudden and unexplained deaths of persons attending a convention of prominent black professionals in San Juan, Puerto Rico. At first believed to be a recurrence of the so-called Legionnaires' disease, it has now been positively diagnosed as sickle cell anemia. How so many persons, confined to a small area, could all be afflicted by this disease remains a mystery. We'll have more on this problem, later in the program, on ABC Special Report."

Mark Hardin looked away from the television set. He felt a growing unease, born of continually frustrated efforts. He had been in Indianapolis for two days now. Nothing had been found on the whereabouts of Armbrewster or Dr. Barr. Their presence, though, could not be doubted. Earlier that afternoon cases of SCA, in steadily growing numbers, began being reported to the city's hospitals. Then, inexplicably, at eight in the evening, the report of new cases ceased as abruptly as it had begun. Still, no trace of Dr. Barr had been found.

Barr's formula left no identifiable residue. This much the Penetrator had learned before leaving Puerto Rico. It was tasteless, odorless, and colorless. And the man, himself, seemed nearly as elusive and invisible as his death spray. The Penetrator simply hadn't enough to take to the authorities. Vulnerable to inquiry and too close an inspection, he dared not expose himself, let alone his unsupported theory, to close scrutiny. Worse yet, to make it public could result in mass hysteria and panic.

Fuming at his sense of helplessness, he reached for the telephone. The least he could do was check in with Captain Jim Nero, see if anything new had gone down.

In a spacious lodge on the Wabash River, outside Lafayette, Indiana, some seventy miles from Indianapolis, Joseph Armbrewster sat in a comfortable leather chair near the hearth. A large blaze roared in the fireplace, dispelling the chill in the high-ceilinged room, as he sipped appreciatively from a hot toddy made with Wild Turkey. He studied his guest over the rim of the copper mug before replying.

"No. I don't agree. We can not afford to go on."

Raymond Barr felt as though he'd received a physical blow. This couldn't happen! All he'd worked for, strived to achieve. A heated protest came from his thin lips.

"B-but we *must*. Don't you see? I hadn't taken into account the diffusing effect of the atmosphere. The *Terminus* was weakened, didn't get them all. There's no assurance that those we despise so were among the victims. We must release another cylinder tomorrow. Only then can we be sure."

Armbrewster tried another tack. "Have you ever heard of a man they call the Penetrator?"

"Y-yes. Some sort of crime fighter. But why worry about him? Brad Lessor told me he was in Puerto Rico."

"Less than twelve hours after you left for here, the Penetrator raided your laboratory. He killed three men Brad left there and utterly destroyed the facilities."

The familiarity with which Armbrewster used Lessor's first name troubled Raymond Barr, but he couldn't put a reason to it. Although shocking, the fact that the lab had been destroyed didn't disturb him as much as this revelation. Given a minimum of equipment, he could produce *Terminus* anywhere now. But what relationship existed between Armbrewster and Brad Lessor? As though reading his mind, Armbrewster answered for Dr. Barr.

"Oh, Brad has worked for me for the past two years."

Suddenly things became clearer for Raymond Barr. He felt used, spied upon. "Then . . . then everything, the commune, Lessor's grand design against the blacks . . . that was all a front?"

"Not all, my dear friend. Our plan to subjugate the niggers, put them back into bondage and out picking cotton where they belong, is quite real." Armbrewster's voice grew hard. "But it has to be done in the proper way and at the proper time. Your little . . . ah, potion is only an added fillip. It is a club we can hold over their heads to keep them in line.

"But, to the immediate situation. Somehow the Penetrator has gotten onto our scheme. That and some other enterprises I was involved in. He hit hard once before and then in Puerto Rico. There's nothing to say that he isn't out there right now, trying to find us and destroy everything before it can be put into effect. I will not have my plans compromised. There can be no further incidents in this area that could result in drawing attention to Indianapolis and to me. You will release *Terminus* only where and when I say to. Is that understood?"

"Yeah . . . I, uh, I suppose I have no other choice. But think of the benefit *Terminus* can have to your plans. By initiating mass deaths among them and then letting it out that it is a plot by whitey, it can bring about the uprising you want so much."

"I have considered that aspect. Rest assured that we will employ *Terminus* in that manner . . . when the time is right."

"What's wrong with right now? Consider New York City. The concentration of their kind is greatest there. It would be ideal."

Thoughts of Stacey flashed through Joseph Armbrewster's mind. Golden girl, beloved daughter, with her first pony, sailing on Lake Michigan, laughing and sparkling beside him in those happy days before that ugly nigger came with his drugs. The anguish of old churned acidly in his belly. Along with his memories came a reflection on the current social and economic conditions.

"You might be right at that," Armbrewster said at last. "The domestic situation can't get any better, and it doesn't seem possible for it to get any worse under the current dim-witted administration. Perhaps it is time to bring on the uprising. Okay. Start laying out plans for New York City."

Chapter 12

A SCORE SETTLED

Jangling jerkily, the hard-driving rhythm of funky music blared from the speaker set above the door to the pool hall on Garven Street, near the center of Indianapolis's downtown ghetto. The stained, littered sidewalk in front swarmed with a sea of black faces. From within the protective darkness of an alley, created by the burning down of a building in some long ago riot, Raymond Barr felt a shiver of danger and discomfort.

They were so many and so close and he was so noticeable and alone. He shook off the feeling of foreboding with a shudder, reminding himself why it was he had come here.

The tip that brought him here turned out to be a valid one. Earlier, through a window, he had recognized the faces of the three men he most hated in his entire life. Hurriedly he had gone to get a cylinder of *Terminus*. Now he made busy, completing his preparations.

Leroy Jackson grinned widely, running his tongue around lips suddenly gone dry. He had run his luck too far. He either must bluff, shake up the opposition, or get out of the game the loser. "Hey, muthuh, a five says I make the combination."

"You on, you jive-ass bastid. Y'all can't make a hole lessin' it's got hair around it."

Frowning in concentration, Leroy leaned one way and then the other, bending low over the green baize field of the pool table. Squinting up his eyes, he took position and addressed the cue ball. Drawing back the blue-chalked tip, he stroked slowly and evenly a couple of times, then hit the white ball a sharp rap. It sped true to its target, cracking between the nine and thirteen ball. Both caromed off toward their indicated pockets.

"Made it, muthuhfucker! Pay me," he shouted, extending his hand. With all eyes on his open palm, Leroy dropped the tip of his cue stick, making a rail along which the thirteen ball ran from its slightly erratic course to drop into the hole.

"Sunbitch, where you learn to shoot pool like that?" the youngster, defeated by Leroy's cheating, asked.

"Juvie Hall, same place you did, turkey. Now, my man, care to wager on the next shot? My last, I might add."

"*Whooeee!* Not me. We got twenny on this game and you done took me fo' another twenny-five. Just go on an' sink that eight and be done with it."

"Cool it," Cleavon "Sugar Man" Bates advised Leroy. "You gonna hustle yourself outta suckers fo' long."

"I dig it, man. We gonna move on from here anyhow, right?"

"Right on," came Amos Petty's voice as he moved closer to the table. "We got us a job laid on and then some soul food and the ladies. Some foxy chick you got waitin' fo' you, Leroy."

"Hey, man, don't go givin' me the hots when I got this im-portant shot to make."

Amos strolled away from the table, stopping beside Sugar Man. "You dig on that dude at the counter?"

Bates's lips curled in contempt and hatred. "Stinkin' pig. Comin' in here makin' out like he was a righteous dude an' all the while keepin' track of the action fo' his honkey bossman. Why can't he be a true brother like the rest of us?"

They continued eyeing the black plainclothes cop while Leroy lined up his eight ball shot. So intent was their study that no one noticed a soft hissing that issued from the end of a length of rubber hose inserted through a slightly opened window.

The Penetrator figured that the mad Doctor Barr had quit his campaign against blacks for some reason. Could it be that the pressure had grown too great? Would Barr move on to some other place, unknown until some forty-eight hours after his fatal visit? How could he find Barr and stop him before that grim scenario had an opportunity to be played out—not once, but perhaps a dozen times?

Mark Hardin spent two fruitless days keeping Joseph Armbrewster's known haunts under surveillance on an irregular schedule. Between times he poked around, gathering all the information he could about Raymond Barr. Stymied, he fumed silently at the frustration of his efforts. Never before had he been made to feel so helpless. Nor had he ever been faced with such an inability to close with the quarry and effect a final solution. Disgruntled, he settled down in his rental car to watch the private entrance to Armbrewster's office building. Idly he reached out to turn on the radio.

"Here's a news bulletin just in to the WIXL newsroom. Public Health officials announced only moments ago that the epidemic of sickle cell anemia that raged through the city a few days ago has apparently flared up again. Over the past six hours twenty-five new cases have been reported to area hospitals. Many were dead on arrival, the others remain on the critical list in terminal condition. Persons of black ethnic background are urged to check with their physicians at once. We'll have more on this event as news breaks."

Mark roused himself, driving to the nearest phone booth where he called Captain Jim Nero.

"I heard about it an hour ago," a worried Jim Nero said into the mouthpiece of his phone.

"Did anything break with it? Anything at all that might tie this in with Armbrewster and Dr. Barr?"

"I was just going over the reports. But . . ." The sound of turning pages came over the phone to the Penetrator's ear. "Wait a minute! Here. Three of those who died before reaching the hospital. Cleavon Bates, Leroy Jackson, and Amos Petty, according to this notification. Those are the three who were involved in the mugging of Dr. Barr and the kidnapping, rape, and murder of his wife."

"So that fits," Mark replied. "Surely, though, no one would develop so dangerous a substance for purely personal revenge? Barr would have to be insane to do that. So would Armbrewster."

"There's nothing that connects Barr with Armbrewster. Neither before nor after Barr's loss. Not that shows, as far as we've been able to dig. As to Barr's stability, I didn't know him prior to his being mugged. Those who did, though, told us he began acting erratically. He started drinking a lot, talked about his wife as though she were only away on a visit somewhere and not dead. No accounting for how all that might have affected his mind."

"*Hmmm,*" the Penetrator mused. "You just said something that might be profound. You say he talked about his wife as though she were still alive?"

"About and *to,* from what I've heard."

"All right. We know Barr was here as recently as two nights ago. You think he might be communing with his wife? I think I know where we can find him. What was her name?"

"Louise. But what? How? . . ." Only Jim Nero found himself talking to a dead line.

"You maniac! You goddamned fool!" Joseph Armbrewster yelled in fury at the cringing figure of Raymond Barr. "What ever possessed you to go after those three?"

"Don't you see? I had to. Without them dead . . . for sure . . . all my efforts would have been in vain. What could I tell her? How could I ever face her without knowing for a fact that they had paid the ultimate penalty?"

"She's *dead*, you imbecile! You can neither see her nor tell her anything, now or ever!"

"But that's not so, you know?" Barr replied, a sly look and tone coming over him. "I see her often. We talk about my work and what it means for us. I promised her, swore on my life, I'd never rest until I'd evened the score for her. And now I've done it. I must go and let her know. She'll be so proud of my accomplishments."

Armbrewster groaned with rage and resignation. "Your mind's turned to mush if you think you can see and converse with a woman who's been buried for five months. Can't you see what danger this has placed us in? Get this straight in your head.

"The Penetrator is on our ass. Nobody knows what he looks like or how to stop him. He doesn't make mistakes, and wherever he goes he leaves a lot of bodies behind him. Now you have to go and advertise that we're here through this idiotic vendetta of yours. Do you know what he did to the three men Lessor left at the lab? While they were alive they burned with white phosphorous. Then he shot them."

Raymond Barr paled, visibly shaken by what he heard. Armbrewster raged on. "We're in some deep shit . . . and getting deeper. Anymore of your cute idiocies and we're not going to be able to dig our way out with a steam shovel.

"It's the booze," Armbrewster went on. "It has to be what rotted your brain. From now on, you're going to have a keeper. We cannot afford another slip."

Crestfallen, Raymond Barr could only nod. At last he stammered out the words. "A-all right. I agree, I agree. I'll do whatever you say. But, first let me go to my wife. Let me tell Louise what I've done. She'll be so proud."

"I'd like everything you have on Dr. Raymond Barr, a Louise Barr, and the trial of Cleavon Bates," the Penetrator told a matronly, efficient-looking woman seated at a small desk in a cubicle created by rows of metal shelves filled with racks of microfilm.

Mark had come to the *Tribune* newspaper morgue as the result of a momentary inspiration. As the woman looked up the references for him, making a list of locations for microfilm spools, he felt a growing impatience. Every minute seemed to count now. If his hunch failed to pay off or he arrived too late, Barr could be gone, anonymous in the mass of two hundred million faces across the nation. Only in grisly retrospect would they know where he'd been. not where to find him. The Penetrator corralled his thoughts as the woman looked up, extending a slip of paper toward him.

"Here you are, sir. You can start in this aisle behind me. I hope you find what you're looking for."

So do I, lady, so do I, the Penetrator thought forcefully as he wandered into the stacks.

Half an hour later he emerged from a viewer cubicle with a look of satisfaction on his face. He'd located what he needed to find Dr. Barr. At least, if his theory proved correct, he would soon have the mad doctor in custody. Thanking the morgue librarian sincerely, Mark headed to the elevators.

Out on the street, the Penetrator climbed into his rented Granada and fired up the engine. His destination was Greenlawn Cemetery, where Louise Barr lay buried and, hopefully, Raymond Barr would appear to visit with his wife.

Chapter 13

CUTTING OFF THE HEAD

"So you see, dear, it has all worked out in the end," Dr. Raymond Barr said, kneeling beside his wife's grave. "These monsters have been punished. No one could deny you that, though some have tried. I was too clever for them.

"Oh, I would have loved to have been there, Louise. To tell them what they were dying of and how they came to get it. What a look of fear would have come into their brutish faces. And I would have laughed. Really I would. But they won't be the last. Together, my dear, we'll get them all." He sat back, pensive.

"Joe Armbrewster is a generous man. But he wants me to stop my great plan. Use *Terminus* only where and when he says to, he ordered me. He wants to give me a guard to see I don't do anything to upset his plans. But that doesn't matter. I'm too clever for them. I'll slip away from them, then together we can go to New York, Chicago, Los Angeles, everywhere with *Terminus* until not a single one of those wretches is left on the face of the earth."

"No, Doctor Barr. It's not going to happen that way."

Raymond Barr looked up to see the Penetrator standing across the grave from him. Mark's dark features were fixed in a scowl that carried a deadly aura about it. With an effort, Dr. Barr tried to shake off the cobra-and-snake attraction the Penetrator seemed to have over him.

"You can't stop me, you know. Nobody can." Barr reached under his coat for a small pistol he had taken to carrying since going to Puerto Rico.

The Penetrator stepped across the grave and dropped Raymond Barr with a solid, stinging backhand blow. The demented biochemist sprawled outward in the thin crust of snow that fringed his wife's gravestone. Mark bent down, searched and disarmed Dr. Barr, then rolled him over and secured his hands behind his back with riot handcuffs. Then he lifted the slightly built man to his feet.

"Come on, Dr. Barr. There are some important people you must talk with."

In that moment, a great change came over Dr. Raymond Barr. White spittle formed and frothed at the corners of his mouth. His eyes went wide and rolled wildly, turning upward into his head, showing only the whites. He began to tremble and mouth meaningless words. Struggling furiously, he sought to escape, but fell into a limp heap when he managed to break Mark's hold. It took all of the Penetrator's strength to keep Dr. Barr under minimum control, and even then he broke loose twice more.

The last time, Mark stooped down and lifted the writhing man into his arms. Then, borne like a child, while howling like a forlorn dog in a graveyard, Dr. Raymond Barr was taken to the car.

"It's no use," Captain Jim Nero said half an hour later. "His mind's snapped completely. Whatever thin shreds of sanity he still possessed have come unglued. We won't be able to get a thing out of him."

"I doubt that he trusted the formula to anyone. With Barr out of the way this should all be over soon. The important thing . . ."

"Is that Barr's been captured, right?" Jim Nero's eyes flashed with anger. "Oh, it's not important how much of that hellish stuff he has lying around for anyone to use. All we have to do is wait until niggers stop dying like flies, something that is definitely *not* important, and then we can rest easy. Isn't that what you . . . ?" Jim Nero stopped before finishing his sentence, silenced by the hurt look that passed over the Penetrator's face.

"I was going to say, before I was interrupted, that the important thing is that we locate any supply Barr had on hand and anyone who knows how to use it . . . and that includes Armbrewster."

Deeply moved, contrite and not fully able to express the shame he felt over his outburst, Jim Nero ran a huge hand over his face, trying to wipe away his self-disgust. "I *am* sorry. Believe me I am. This thing is getting me down. Tearing right into my guts. Having to live with the possibility that it could happen to my wife, my kids . . . God help me, *to me*. I thought, after all I've gone through, I was immune to self-pity." He tried a weak smile. "I see I'm not. Forgive my intemperance, will you?"

The Penetrator placed a consoling hand on the big detective's shoulder. "It's all right. I know where you're coming from, Jim. But my job's still not finished. I'm going after Armbrewster and the rest."

"You know, Brad, the more I think about it, the more I become convinced that Barr has the right idea," Joe Armbrewster told Brad Lessor when the latter came to the remote fishing lodge. "Particularly with the Penetrator mixed into it."

"The guy's bad news, all right. The thing I can't figure out is how he got on to us."

"You remember the fishing conglomerate? Apparently someone complained loud and long in the right places, and the next thing you know the Penetrator shows up. He shook up some of the muscle I sent down there and damn near destroyed the Baymaster shipyard."

"Never could understand why you wanted to get mixed up in that."

Armbrewster chuckled softly. "Call it a little vanity of mine. I love seafood, but the prices are getting so high that even I can't afford all the oysters and scallops I want. So I figured to get me a wholesale company of my own. Once I had a processing plant, and I already owned a shipyard, I thought why not go all the way. There's a lot of money in that business, and this way I'd be the one making it instead of spending it." He took a sip of his drink. "Or at least that's what I tried to convince myself of. It's all a matter of power, Brad. Money and power. I want the niggers on their knees where they belong. But that takes engineering a revolution. And equipping an army, fomenting a revolution, these are things that would tax the resources of Armbrewster Steel far too greatly. Most of my wealth is on paper: tied up in property, buildings, machinery, raw materials and finished product. There's always the chance the plan might fail and I don't want to liquidate all my assets on a gamble. The more sources of outside income I have the better the chance of bringing this off."

"But all it resulted in was getting the Penetrator into the middle of things."

"Only too true, Brad, much to my regret. I fear I

moved too far, too fast. I built Armbrewster Steel with patience and careful planning. But since Stacey . . . died, I seem to have run out of patience. We're so close. With Barr's formula we have a chance of pulling it off."

"Meanwhile we have to find the Penetrator and fix his clock."

"If he's around, he'll find us. What you need to be sure of is being able to deal with him swiftly and finally.

"Now, Barr said something about New York City," Armbrewster went on, returning to the main topic. "Where is he, by the way?"

"I don't know. He never showed at the wish store. I thought he might be out here."

"No. Damn that man. First he defies my order about not using the stuff again, then he disappears. Oh, well, he'll show up sooner or later, if he hasn't lost what little sanity he has left. It might be that we'll have to remove this minor irritant. But to get back to important things.

"Let's lay solid plans for releasing the gas in New York City. It should serve as a diversion, draw the Penetrator off from this area. Perhaps then Detroit, Chicago, New Orleans, the Deep South . . ." Armbrewster's voice droned on, speaking calmly and seemingly rationally about a reign of horror beyond any sane man's imagination.

Raymond Barr remained under sedation in the psychiatric ward of the general hospital. Massive dosages of the tranquilizer, Thorazine, were required to keep him from doing harm to himself and reduce his raving. Three days after his capture, the Penetrator and the Police were no closer to learning where he had hidden his supply of the deadly serum than when Mark had apprehended him at Louise Barr's grave. After another fruitless visit, the Penetrator felt a nagging conviction that he was merely spinning his wheels.

Armbrewster. It all had to revolve around Joseph Armbrewster and whatever scheme he had devised that required the ability to kill blacks—and only blacks—at will. Somehow, Mark felt sure, the attempt to take over the Gulf Coast fishing industry played a part in it as well. By the time he reached police headquarters, the Penetrator had replayed the scant list of facts often enough to make them sound meaningless.

"Did you see this morning's paper?" Jim Nero asked as Mark slumped into a chair opposite the detective's desk.

"No. I've been kicking around what we know and what we suspect, trying to come up with some lead on Armbrewster."

"Look at this! It's incredible. New York, Chicago, Detroit . . . all in the last three days. Somehow, even without Barr, Armbrewster's been able to spread the thing over half the country. My God, every black person in the nation is living in fear. Something new's been added. See this," Captain Nero said, handing Mark the paper. "Whoever did it left messages behind. They claim it is being done as part of the whiteman's revenge on troublemakers, welfare bums, and uppity blacks. And they say this is only the start. If this keeps on, someone's bound to take them seriously and we'll be in for more riots like those in the sixties."

"That's it!"

"What do you mean?"

When I interrogated one of the Scum of the Earth in San Juan, he started raving about some plan of Lessor's to get a black revolution going and then wind up as absolute dictator. It sounded like the wild ramblings of Charles Manson, so I discounted it at the time as some sort of shuck Lessor used to keep his collection of nuts together. Now I'm not so sure. That sort of thing takes money and planning. It could be what was behind that grab for power in Mississippi. It's Armbrewster, not Lessor, who plans on taking over after the bloodbath."

"It's crazy. But I think you have something there. Armbrewster's rich, he's used to wielding power . . . and he's ambitious. I can even see him viewing it as a means of exacting enormous revenge for what happened to Stacey . . . his daughter." Nero's tone changed.

"Look, I'd offer you a badge, but I have a feeling you wouldn't accept it. I don't know what your involvement in this happens to be and, when it comes to that, I don't even know who you really are. I'm relying on Willard Haskins's endorsement when I say for you to run with this thing. But chasing down motive and verifying it doesn't tell us where to look for them. Any ideas on that?"

"Now I have. Where would you go to get a thing like this started? It's the one place we haven't looked for Armbrewster and Lessor."

"Where's that?"

"In the heart of the black ghetto, of course."

Jim Nero's face went blank. "Well, I'll be damned."

Marla Ayers nudged her partner. "There, Billy. That one comin' down the steps. He's the guy from Puerto Rico."

"You're right, Marl. Sure as hell is." Billy started forward, but Marla grabbed his arm, holding him back.

"Hold on. We gotta see where he goes, what he's up to."

"Yeah. I'll go tell Brad we've found him. You keep on his tail and call in to let us know where he went."

"Right on." The girl began following the tall, broad-shouldered man.

His mind busy fitting the facts to his new theory, the Penetrator turned the opposite direction from the scraggly pair and headed down the street to where he'd parked his car. He seemed completely unaware that he was being followed.

Chapter 14

WISHES FOR SALE

No one really liked the honkeys that ran the wish store. What business did they have coming into Decatur Street and selling soul stuff? But then the dude with the red Afro and far-out funky clothes had a cool way of interpreting dreams. He claimed to be a Gypsy and everyone knew Gypsies had to have a touch of the tar brush. They couldn't be so good at telling fortunes and explaining dreams if they didn't. Besides the whiteys sold good herbs and incense, tarot cards, ju-ju beads, and other things that were hard to get.

They also sold some mighty fine dreams of their own from the back room. Only the best quality hash, acid, coke, and angel dust. So, the Muskrat Den wish shop did a good business.

Complete in his "business" regalia of wildly colored robes, covered by cabalistic symbols, and two-inch-soled half-Wellingtons, his hair bleached and teased into a fluffy red-orange Afro, Brad Lessor leaned back, tilting onto the rear legs of the chair he occupied. A rap session was going on, everyone having snorted a little coke on the house.

Lessor enjoyed listening to these sessions. He felt smugly superior to those around him. Surprisingly he didn't feel the least discomfited by his surroundings. All this was transient, he thought triumphantly. Before long the niggers would be back in the cotton fields where they belonged. Thank God for Adolph Hitler, who showed the way!

While languishing in Joliet prison, Brad Lessor had had opportunity to read *Mein Kampf*. He found the racial paranoia of Hitler appealing and somehow a justification for his previous sense of inferiority. Mostly self-educated since high school, Lessor applied the twisted reasoning of the mad Austrian to society as he viewed it. Someone, he contended, was putting the skids to the United States. Probably not the Jews, as Hitler had claimed, but some group. He, like everyone else, had become their victims. Looking back on the Civil Rights movement and the student violence of the sixties had given him his answer. The blacks, he convinced himself, had to be behind it.

When he gained release from prison, Lessor gravitated to the Nazis around Skokie, Illinois. He rose in their ranks until he learned that one of the secret contributors to their treasury was Joseph T. Armbrewster. Armed with this information, he headed for Indianapolis. He met with Armbrewster and they talked. Once they reached agreement on a mutual philosophy, Armbrewster hired Brad Lessor on the spot. He learned that Armbrewster was not, himself, a Nazi. No, the steel magnate had a far more ambitious plan and a personal desire to be the power behind the throne. His support of the Skokie Brown Shirts was only one element of insuring his desire. He also gave money to the Black Panthers, the Ku Klux Klan, and the extremist Black Liberation Coalition. What Armbrewster wanted was a race war.

The more he thought of it, the better Lessor liked the idea. Together they worked out details of the plan, including sources for financing arms and explosives for those who would carry revolution into the streets. Lessor had been sent in during the early stages of taking over the fishing industry and had left Gulf Port only a week before the Penetrator arrived to clean house. He had been called back to oversee the operations of Dr. Raymond Barr.

Now Lessor had the formula and enough *Terminus* to insure terror could be released when and where it was wanted. It didn't matter to him that Barr had somehow disappeared. Who needed the boozy little creep? Providing tender flesh for the horny scientist's tastes had become a problem for Lessor. Particularly since Barr demanded ever younger girls following each orgy, until they'd reached the preteen-age group—with few willing volunteers—at the time when Armbrewster summoned them back to Indianapolis. Maybe the old goat had found him some precocious ten-year-old with as insatiable a lust as his own and was shacked up somewhere. His reflections were interrupted by the arrival of Billy.

"Hey, man. We've found him."

"Who, Barr?" Lessor demanded.

"Naw. You know, that Penetrator guy."

"You're kidding. How'd he know to come here?" Lessor said lightly, but the revelation troubled him. He mobilized his troops, moving into a small office and summoning several Scum members.

"We've got to hit this dude right this time. Billy tells me that Marla is following him and will check in when he lights somewhere. We've got a couple of MP-40s that Armbrewster got us for the spades.

We're gonna chop the Penetrator up in little pieces." Lessor continued laying plans, waiting for Marla to telephone.

How could it have happened? One moment Marla had been following the Penetrator after he'd parked his car at the edge of the city park, the next second he seemed to fade out and disappear. Things like that couldn't be, could they? She'd had no difficulty so far, his broad back and tall, smoothly moving body was easy to spot even a block away. So how did he pull his vanishing act?

Marla increased her pace, closing on the last place she knew she had seen the Penetrator. Ah! That's the answer, she thought, as she noticed a small path opening in the brush and beyond the stone front of a restroom building. He'd turned in here. As she edged her way up the narrow track, a powerful arm snaked around her chest and jerked her off her feet. A big hand clamped over her mouth prevented her from screaming. Struggling was futile, she soon discovered. The guy carried her as though her hundred and ten pounds were nothing. Before she realized what had happened, he dumped her on the cold cement floor of the men's room.

Quickly the Penetrator secured Marla's hands and feet with nylon parachute cord. So far her reaction to being abducted had kept her from screaming, so Mark bent close to give her an additional reason.

"Make any noise other than to answer questions and I'll cut your throat from ear to ear."

Marla's mind, somewhat fogged by the coke she'd been snorting, worked as best it could. Maybe she could run a bluff. "You lousy bastard. Are you one of those rape killers that's in the papers all the time?"

The Penetrator grinned, a gesture of grim irony.

"Come on. You know who I am. Now I want to know why you were following me."

"You son-of-a-bitch, I wasn't following anyone."

"My, my. Such unlady-like language becomes you so. From the looks of you and that mouth of yours, I'd say you were one of the Scum of the Earth."

Marla's eyes widened. God, was this guy psychic or something? Startled into silence again, she remained quiet, which gave Mark an opportunity to examine his captive.

He had a real problem on his hands. From the looks of her eyes and that red nose she had probably recently taken some sort of drug. Coke or speed, not heroin at least. But that still made it impossible to get information the easy way. No telling what reaction might be set off by using a truth serum. Harsh words were not likely to get her tongue wagging either. That left torture and he couldn't bring himself to exercise the grisly art on a girl. But if she *thought* she might be tortured . . .

Mark bent down and placed a gag in Marla's mouth, put a quickly lettered OUT OF ORDER sign on the restroom door, and went about setting the stage for his interrogation. He returned a few minutes later, but did not take out the knotted handkerchief that filled Marla's mouth. Squatting beside her he began talking while breaking up small twigs and thin branches he had carried in.

"I'd hoped we could do this the easy way. We could have, too, if you hadn't been stupid enough to get half-stoned on something or other. So it has to be the hard way.

"Torture is a refined art these days. They use cattle prods, magnetos rigged to various tender parts of your body. But I haven't any of the sophisticated things along. I'll have to rely on more primitive methods. The Native Americans were great for those sort of things.

"They came up with all sorts of clever ways of extracting information from captives." Mark watched Marla's eyes closely for the first signs of genuine fear. He reached out and opened her coat and roughly pulled up her shirt, laying bare the soft skin of her belly. "One of the most devilishly ingenious schemes was dreamed up by the Apache. They used to build a small fire of tiny sticks on their victim's stomach. Not a roaring blaze, you see, merely enough to keep burning. Then they'd add one stick at a time until it got hot enough to roast its way through the person's flesh. You'd be surprised how many answers they could get that way."

While he explained the torture, the Penetrator had laid a small fire on Marla's stomach. Now he produced a kitchen match from his coat pocket and struck it on the floor. He held it so that the girl could see its flame. Her eyes darted wildly about, proclaiming the state of terror that ravaged her mind. As best she could, she thrashed about, dislodging the small tent of twigs and throwing them from her body.

"Ready to answer my questions, are you?" Mark put an evil grin on his face and leaned forward to remove the gag. "Good. I felt sure you might be induced to cooperate. Now, let's start with your name. It's nice to know with whom one is speaking."

In ten brief minutes Marla had told the Penetrator everything, including the location of Brad Lessor and the rest of the Scum, and information about the hit team that was to be sent out. As to her phone call, the Penetrator had an idea of his own. He raised the girl to her feet, cut the cords, and, after her circulation was restored, hustled her out of the building and down a lane to a public phone booth.

Under the Penetrator's instructions, Marla contacted Lessor and told him that the Penetrator was in the city park. She said she'd keep an eye on him until they arrived. After hanging up, the Penetrator put another coin in the slot and dialed a number.

He told Captain Jim Nero about the hit team and where to scoop them up. Then he said to look in the men's room with the OUT OF ORDER sign on the door for Marla. All in all he felt pleased with his small surprise for the Scum of the Earth.

Chapter 15

DOUBLE HEADER

Oowiee! If the action at the Muskrat Den wish store hadn't been memorable enough, how it came apart would be stored in the memory of every brother and sister in Indianapolis. Some twenty-five or thirty righteous dudes were out on the streets when this big honkey pulls up in a car, gets out holding a funny-lookin' submachine gun, and begins to disassemble the place.

The Penetrator hadn't planned his raid on the Scum of the Earth wish store so that he had nearly half a hundred witnesses, it simply happened that way. Time alone dictated his midafternoon strike, and time, he believed, had nearly run out. His face grim, he strode across the sidewalk and raised one foot to kick in the door.

Len Daley looked up from behind the counter as the front door of the Muskrat Den crashed inward. He saw a dark figure silhouetted in the outside sun glare off a newly fallen snow, and started to mouth a protest. Then items on a shelf behind him and above his head began to disintegrate. Len ducked low, wondering why he had not heard any explosions from the gun this stranger must be carrying. He made no attempt at defense, his face pressed into the rough, dirty floorboards. The invader fired several more silent bursts and started to walk through the store. Len tried to dig a hole in the boards with frightened fingers.

The Penetrator headed unerringly toward the bead-curtain-covered entrance to the back room. His silenced Sidewinder nestled comfortably along his right forearm. When he reached his objective he hazarded a quick glance inside.

Frozen in startled positions of half-rising, five persons hovered around a large table. As the Penetrator's head popped back out of sight, two Scum members dived for a cupboard where four sawed-off shotguns reposed. Brad Lessor and the remaining pair drew handguns, firing wildly through the opening, breaking beads and one front plate glass window, but not harming their attacker. Then the Penetrator shoved the fat muzzle of the MAC silencer into the room and fired two short bursts.

Objects shattered noisily, slugs moaned and whined off metal storage racks and the five Scum of the Earth hit the floor. One shotgun blasted double-aught pellets through the wall where the Penetrator should have been. Brad Lessor suddenly realized that there were a lot of places far better to be than the Muskrat Den wish store. Pointing silently he positioned his troops.

Billy and the other man were to cover the front with their shotguns while Lessor sent one man to check the alley exit. He and Sammy Ney—who'd first spotted the Penetrator in Puerto Rico—remained in the center of the room, upending the table in classic B-Western style to act as a barricade. Had those actors from whom Lessor absorbed his early gunfighting tactics been using even the low-power, black powder rounds available in the frontier era in their blank-loaded .45 Long Colts, they would have cut through thick tabletops like hungry mice in well-aged cheese. This fact seemed to have escaped Lessor's later learning process. But, as the Penetrator appeared briefly in the doorway, he disabused the Scum of the Earth leader of his false security.

Three 185-grain, jacketed hollowpoint slugs noisily drill-pressed their way through the heavy oak table. Sammy cried out, falling back and clutching his bleeding left shoulder. The shotguns boomed far too late and Lessor had a decision to make.

"Keep him busy," Lessor yelled, jumping to his feet and making a dash for the back of the building.

One of the shotgunners grew careless in his anxiety to end this unexpected threat. He leaped into the open and cranked out three more rounds from his '97 Winchester pump. Beads, plaster, and lathe flew like shrapnel as the pellets did their only damage. The Sidewinder in Mark Hardin's hand spat three more .45 slugs that stitched the incautious gunman across his chest.

As the big lead chunks mushroomed inside the Scum soldier's body, bursting his heart, smashing tissue and pulverizing a section of spinal column, Brad Lessor grabbed up three small cylinders of *Terminus* and, half-dragging Sammy, made a dash out into the alley to freedom. Behind him, Billy's shotgun boomed, he screamed in agony, and the Penetrator's footsteps pounded over the rough board floor.

Mark reached the alley in time to see Lessor disappearing onto the street, driving a metallic-blue short-bed Chevy pickup. The Penetrator made a quick sprint back through the store, dispersing for a moment the crowd gathered outside with the menacing appearance of his SMG, and fired up his rental Granada. Two blocks away he could still see the azure gleam of Lessor's truck cab.

Lessor skillfully threaded his way through the ghetto section of Indianapolis and took the first available on-ramp to the South bypass. He opened up the little truck then, roaring along 475, past I-70 and US-36. Moments later, right behind him, the Penetrator flashed along the cement strip, going by the Indianapolis Speedway. Engaged in a discreet speed contest of his own, Mark thought briefly of how he could make good use of one of those 185-mph-plus cars that annually pounded the brick course for people's Memorial Day entertainment. Ahead of him, Lessor disappeared down a ramp onto I-65.

Traffic thinned out as they left Indianapolis behind. Thundering down the highway they passed the Lebanon and Frankfort turnoffs, heading northwest. At the Lafayette interchange, Lessor turned off onto State 25, racing northeast toward Delphi. Behind him, the Penetrator struggled to close the gap.

It became obvious to Mark that Lessor's truck had been equipped with parts far from standard, as the 1959 pickup maintained its steady lead. As they ran along parallel to the Wabash River, the Penetrator cursed the unresponsive, underpowered performance of the idiotic unleaded fuel engine in the Granada as Lessor's considerable lead began to widen. He longed for the rumbling ponies of his full-blown 300 Chrysler hemi under the hood of his '57 Chevy, or the brute strength of the powerhouse in his Brown Beast Ford pickup. Doomed to endure the less than adequate power-to-weight ratio of the Granada, he floorboarded the accelerator.

As the Penetrator began to eat up some of the vast distance between him and the fleeing Lessor, the pickup braked sharply and turned onto a narrow macadam lane. The Penetrator negotiated the same corner and strove again to cut down Lessor's lead. As he sped down the blacktop, Mark noticed the tall fieldstone columns of a symbolic gateway, and a large sign reading; WABASH CLIFF ESTATES. Sight of it gave him a feeling of relief and satisfaction. Flushing Lessor had led him to Armbrewster. It had to be.

"Goddammit! The Penetrator's right on my tail," Lessor yelled at a startled Joseph Armbrewster, who stood on his doorstep at the lodge.

"What did you lead him here for?"

"There's no place else to go and I had to protect the supply of *Terminus*."

"Get in here, then."

Inside the high-ceilinged, glass-walled living room, Armbrewster went to a radio set on a sideboard. He picked up the mike and spoke tersely into it. "I'm expecting an uninvited guest. Make sure he doesn't reach the front door."

"Rog-o on that, Boss," came the reply. Armbrewster turned back to a shaken Brad Lessor.

"Now, let's hear it from the top."

Lessor explained about one of his men spotting the Penetrator, of the tail put on him, and the hit team sent out. He concluded with the raid on the wish store. Afterward he gratefully accepted the drink Armbrewster offered.

"Looks like you screwed it up good, Brad. Any suggestions on what to do now?"

"Stop him. Just for God's sake stop the bastard."

"A not so easy proposition I'd say," Armbrewster remarked calmly as they heard from outside the muffled sound of gunshots, excited, yelling voices, and the roar of an engine in low gear.

Although wounded, Sammy was able to handle the MP-40 submachine gun Brad Lessor had left with him in the cab of the pickup. He looked up cautiously as he listened to the sound of the approaching Granada. Leaning out the side window he released a ten-round burst that disintegrated the windshield of the careening vehicle. That had to have done in that son-of-a-bitch Penetrator.

Sammy's hopes crumbled as he saw the Granada veer to one side and aim directly at the Chevy truck. Yelling in fright, Sammy scrambled across the seat toward the driver's door. His hand had barely touched the handle when the Granada broadsided the pickup.

Impact catapaulted Sammy out the door, head and shoulders through the rolled-up window and the remainder of his body whipping around the resisting narrow edge, as the frame sprang and the door flew outward. Sammy's spine broke, ending the scream that bubbled out of his slit throat. The Penetrator dived from the car as the Granada's momentum continued, pushing into the peeling metal of the truck, shoving it up and over onto two wheels.

Gasoline from the ruptured tank spilled out, vaporizing and bursting into flames on the hot metal of the Granada's engine. Sammy would never feel the fire of his cremation, but the Penetrator had to move fast to avoid the conflagration. As he rolled away into the clear, three men burst from the woods.

In the center of the trio stood a uniformed man. As the others brought up their weapons, he held out a cautioning hand. "Hold it, don't shoot. It's just one man."

"The boss's orders were to see he never got to the house," the burly man on his right replied, swinging up his Universal M-1 Carbine.

The Penetrator had centered the front post of his

Star PD on the uniformed man, believing him to be the leader, but now changed targets in barely enough time to get in the first shot. His slug smashed into the 30-round magazine of the carbine, wrenching it violently in the receiver well, making the weapon inoperative. The gunman dropped the useless piece and clawed under his heavy winter coat for a pistol as the Penetrator rolled to one side and fired again.

Mark's bullets came a little late, allowing the second guard to snap off two rounds from his Ruger .44 Mag. carbine. The fat, high-velocity slugs tore up fountains of snow and frozen turf ahead and to the left of where the Penetrator lay. Then the Penetrator's bullets zipped in to make a figure-eight-shaped third eye in the gunman's forehead. He rocked back on his heels and partially raised his weapon again, then toppled backward in slow motion to stain the snow with his blood and brains. The Penetrator turned his attention back to the man with the damaged carbine.

A Charter Arms Bulldog snarled fiercely as three .357 rounds whirred through space near the Penetrator's ear. He fired too quickly, the bullet entering the gunman's right thigh, staggering him and causing the shooter to drop his revolver and sit down suddenly. That made Mark's second slug go high, opening a nearly half-inch-wide furrow through the top of the man's skull and spilling out his brains as he fell backward in limp, spasming death. Looking around, the Penetrator dicovered that during the brief firefight, the uniformed man had fled the scene.

The Penetrator climbed to his feet, glad that the other guard had departed. Like most security guards, the man no doubt didn't receive enough pay to die for his employer. If he came from a legitimate company, chances were he wasn't even armed. Going into an uncharted combat zone, the Penetrator's greatest worry always centered around the possibility of harming some innocent person. This desertion of the field eliminated his chance of injuring one of the sheep. Crackling flames drew Mark's attention back to his ruined car.

The Granada was roiling in flames; the doors, trunk, and hood sprang open. The Penetrator had only time to rush to the flaming vehicle and retrieve his suitcase of arms. One arm up to shield his face from the heat, the Penetrator backed away from the wrecked vehicles, feeling singed hair crinkle up, and smelling sickly sweet odor of burning flesh as Sammy got an earthly preview of his eternal condition. He took out a concussion grenade and then used his Star PD to shoot out a sizable hole in one of the house's plate glass windows. Pulling the pin, he tossed the hand bomb into Joseph T. Armbrewster's living room.

Brad Lessor stood in the rear hallway while Armbrewster worked frantically at the safe in his study, stuffing money into an open attaché case. When the concussion grenade went off, wrecking furniture, blowing out windows in a tinkling cascade of glass shards, and bringing down plaster and dust from between the exposed ceiling beams, Lessor blacked out for a moment, his ears ringing fiercely and a dizzying feeling on the verge of nausea sweeping through his body. Armbrewster came from his office, whimpering in pain and bleeding from one ear.

"Let's get out of here. My God, Brad, how can one man be so fierce?"

They struggled out the back, toward the garage, as the Penetrator assaulted the locked and bolted front door.

Mark shot away the round brass cylinder of the deadbolt and, after changing magazines, perforated the regular lock case, kicking in the wide oak panel. He dived through the doorway, gun at the ready, only to be met by emptiness. Coming to his feet he began a hurried, but cautious, search of the fishing lodge.

In the living room, grown cold now from the missing windows, Mark found another of the plain-clothes, tough-looking guards. He lay unconscious on the floor, bleeding from both ears and his mouth. The Penetrator moved on, seeking the elusive Joseph Armbrewster and Brad Lessor. He'd found the open safe in Armbrewster's study when he heard the whirring zipper sound of studded snow tires on the icy driveway and the roar of an engine as Armbrewster's Lincoln labored to gain momentum.

He dashed to the kitchen in time to fire three shots into the trunk deck and right rear wheel well before the Mark V disappeared around the corner of the house. Try as he might, the range had grown too great when Mark reached the front door. Now he had a problem in finding functional transportation and continuing the chase.

A two-minute search widened Armbrewster's lead, but provided Mark with one of the security type's Cobra. Firing up the hot little car, the Penetrator went in pursuit of the fleeing mass murderers. By the time he gained visual contact with the big black car, he realized his chase would be a long one.

Retracing the route between the lodge and Indianapolis provided constant frustration. The Penetrator was forced to reduce speed and lose sight of his quarry three times because of highway patrol cars, parked along the median strip, who were "taking pictures" and "giving out green-stamps" as the CBers would call it. The big Lincoln had flown past them doing well over eighty. Funny that none of the troopers had raised a hair about that. Perhaps, here in Indiana, too, some were considered more equal than others.

Mark fretted through his enforced periods of legal fifty-five miles per hour each time, then let the needle creep upward toward eighty-five as soon as the gumball-machine patrol car tops disappeared behind. Even so, only the greatest of skill and luck combined to let the Penetrator get a glimpse of Armbrewster's Mark V as it whipped down an off-ramp outside the Indianapolis airport. On the surface streets, the Penetrator's task became even more difficult.

The Penetrator slithered between large trucks making deliveries and a clogging stream of passenger cars. With the weather as rotten as it had been, why didn't these people stay home? He continued down a wide street until ahead of him the Continental pulled into a parking lot attached to one of the general aviation hangars. He found a slot in time to park and leave his car, while he watched Armbrewster and Lessor pass through a gate in the low chain-link fence and disappear up the steps into a Lear Jet, which stood on the ramp, one engine fired up, waiting to taxi out.

The Penetrator made it to the gate as the Lear increased its turbine whine to a piercing twin-engine shriek, and rolled smoothly out toward the active runway. Frustrated, helpless, Mark stood a moment before turning away. Without credentials and a lot of explaining he could never get the tower to order the biz jet back to the ramp before it would be off and away. He made a careful note of the registration number and entered the building.

"Here you are, sir. Lear Four-Two-Six-Four Whiskey filed an IFR flight plan for Miami, Florida. Two passengers and a crew of three," the man behind the counter said, reading off the stiff white card that held a copy of the pilot's flight plan. "Mr.

Armbrewster's parked his jet here since he first got it," he volunteered.

"Thanks," the Penetrator said glumly and headed for where his Mooney was hangared out of the weather.

In ten minutes, the Penetrator had pulled away the wheel chocks and a line boy had attached a yoke to the nose wheel studs. As the huge telescoping doors rolled back, Mark entered the office, called Flight Service for the weather, then filed an IFR flight plan to Macon, Georgia. When he returned to the Mooney, now standing squat and speedy-looking on the ramp, he found he had company.

"I figured you wouldn't be far behind our mutual friend," Jim Nero said laconically. "So I thought I'd better be here to detain you so we don't have a lot more bodies scattered over the countryside."

"I'm following Armbrewster, yes, but I don't know what you're talking about on the other."

"It took me awhile to figure it out, but now I know who you are." At Mark's raised eyebrow, he continued. "Though I can't figure out what Willard Haskins is doing associated with the Penetrator."

"The Penetrator! You're out of your tree, Nero."

"Save the denials for someone else. Dr. Barr recovered enough under tranquilizers to tell us that the Penetrator was after him and Armbrewster, and that it was the Penetrator who captured him. Now no one is necessarily going to believe everything a nut tells him. But then we hear about this place down on Decatur Street getting knocked over, two guys dead and a bunch of blue flint arrowheads laying around. Now, that's bad enough under any circumstances, yet the next thing happens, we get a routine notification from up north a ways. Seems someone wasted a pair of Armbrewster's goon-type bodyguards, burned up a couple of vehicles, and took off chasin' Armbrewster. Again some arrowheads left around, and the description of the guy who did it, according to the Jane's Security Service guard who phoned it in, matches you point perfect."

"Look, Jim, while you're standing here chasing a wild goose, that Lear is getting further ahead of me. It makes damn near three times the speed of my Mooney."

"We'll let the law take care of it on the other end. Okay? Whatever his reasons, Willard Haskins has thrown in his lot with you. That's good enough for me. I'm not going to detain you and hand you over to the feds. As it is, I happen to like what you do, even if you skirt close to the other side of the fence from time to time. But I can't knowingly let you go after Armbrewster when the consequences can only lead to more bloodshed."

Mark smiled deprecatingly, making a helpless, apologetic gesture. "Sorry, Jim, but there isn't a hell of a lot you can do to stop me."

"Yes there is." Captain Jim Nero made what seemed only the slightest of movements, but defter than the magic of Doug Henning, a .38 Chief's Special appeared in his hand. The muzzle centered unwaveringly on the Penetrator's chest.

Chapter 16

TWO GUNS ARE BETTER THAN ONE

Looking at the muzzle of Captain Nero's revolver the Penetrator realized he faced no real threat. He could drop the black cop in any of a dozen ways. But his careful conditioning to never endanger the life of an honest policeman stood in the way. Furthermore, he didn't want to hurt this man he had grown to admire greatly. Even the simplest of disarming moves invited, at the least, a broken finger. The longer he waited, the higher the risk.

With reflexes even swifter than the black detective's, Mark lashed out and batted Nero's gun arm into the air. The Penetrator stepped in then, turning Jim Nero away from him and abandoning the fancy martial arts moves for a good old-fashioned half-Nelson. With his left hand he reached out and plucked the .38 revolver from Jim's helpless hand.

"Sorry about that, Jim, but I want Armbrewster and no one's going to get in my way. I'm going to have to tie you up and tuck you away in a corner of that hangar over there."

"Hey, look, man. I want him even more than you do. It's *my* people he's wastin', *my* people he wants to get into a suicidal race war. My gut burns every minute that son-of-a-bitch is walkin' around alive and free. You got me now, but what are you going to do with me?"

"What do you mean?"

"You can't leave me here alive. You gotta kill me or I'll see you get busted the first time you land for gas. That means you have to take me along. If I'm goin', I might as well go in a way that can do you the most good." Despite the pain in his shoulder from the hold the Penetrator still applied, the black detective smiled. "Besides, two guns are better than one, right?"

The Penetrator gave it a brief second's thought. Then he released Nero and handed him back his revolver, after emptying it of its ammunition. "I'll buy that. But this thing is liable to get bloody before it's over. And wherever we end up, you'll have no more jurisdiction than I have."

"So what? You buyin' that, too?"

"I've already bought it. Let's go."

Seven and a half hours later, the Penetrator had learned that Jim Nero had a little difficulty with IFR charts, but he was a competent pilot with some two hundred hours beyond his private license, and fond of Polack jokes. They were also approaching Miami for a second refueling stop. By radio, the Penetrator discovered that 4264W had refiled in flight, naming their new destination as San Juan, Puerto Rico. On the ground, while the Mooney had its tanks topped off, Mark and Jim Nero grabbed cold sandwiches and cans of hot beef stew in the lounge, filled a half-gallon thermos with coffee, and settled down for a brief rest while studying the charts for the islands.

Calle Cortez, one of the scummier back streets of San Juan, held a certain attraction for persons engaged in a variety of activities not countenanced by the law. Brad Lessor left Joseph Armbrewster at the Hotel San Juan, awaiting the arrival by commercial airline of a contingent of his bodyguards, and headed to No. 29 Cortez Street an hour after they landed in Puerto Rico.

"Jose, Bernardo, Sequin, Ramon," Lessor began in excellent Spanish, "I trust you four more than all the others in the liberation movement. What I'm going to ask you hasn't anything to do with making Puerto Rico a separate nation. What I need is an army. Soldiers who will fight if necessary, but who will probably only be called on to act as a screening force until one particular man is identified and taken care of. Can I rely on your people to support me?"

A chorus of agreement rose from around the rickety table in the rear of the cantina. Quickly, Lessor then gave each man his instructions. When the last of the revolutionaries had departed, Lessor also left, heading for another meeting.

Under the railroad bridge on the spur line leading to the Bacardi factory, at a spot on the dry Rio Piedras, far removed from the splendid campus of the University of Puerto Rico, Lessor met with a far different group. Here the ragamuffin victims of the island's crushing overpopulation had an unofficial headquarters. Standing around the tall *gringo* in their tattered clothes, their skinny bodies grime-encrusted by years of inattention, the leaders of the street urchin gangs listened as Lessor described the Penetrator.

"So if any of you or your followers see a man who looks like that at the airport or anywhere on the streets, come to me at once and tell me where he is. Have several boys follow him so we'll know where to find him. There'll be money and rum and a lot of food laid on for you if you succeed. Everyone will have a share in the fiesta, not just those who find this man. Agreed?"

The boys, ranging from eleven to sixteen, welcomed the idea of making money. They considered this assignment an adventure rather than work—which they scorned—and looked forward to the promised rewards. Even as Lessor cautioned them to be careful, they scattered in all directions to locate their loosely associated groups of from six to twenty boys. Smiling confidently, Lessor returned to make his report to Armbrewster.

"I like it, Brad. You've put this thing together under the most trying circumstances. When do we leave for this farm of yours?"

"Farm? Oh, yeah, the commune. You never did get out to see that, did you?"

"I thought it best to keep our association as secret as possible."

"Right on. Well, I have to say it is perfect. Right by the beach, all laid out so that no one would believe there was anything going on but what they could see. I studied photographs of Manson's setup and the layout of Jonestown, sort of built the place along the best lines of both. Before a week was up every scruffy long-haired creep on the island was flocking to join the movement. Those six hard guys you sent along to keep an eye on the Doc just got lost in the crowd."

"Fine. Perhaps if I'd kept your organizing abilities in Gulfport . . ." Armbrewster speculated aloud. Then he returned to the subject. "If everything is organized here, then we can leave in the morning. My bodyguards are due in on a flight at seven this evening."

"Yeah. We can use them. And we'll need some chow, a vehicle for transportation, a few essentials, but I'll have it all rounded up by eight-thirty in the morning."

The Penetrator took a more direct route to San Juan this time, stopping to top off the tanks in Nassau and heading across water to Puerto Rico. They arrived an hour before dawn and headed for a much-needed sleep. As they left the airport, three pair of ancient and knowing eyes in young bodies marked the fact and scurried to earn their reward.

"We leave now," Armbrewster decided when Lessor had translated the rapid-fire Spanish of the small street urchin, who stood just inside the doorway to the suite.

"Give me half an hour. As it is, we'll be lucky to get a car big enough to haul everyone." Lessor handed a twenty-dollar bill to the boy, patted him on the head, and ushered him out into the hall. Returning, he observed with some unease that a pallor had come to Armbrewster's skin and his hands trembled slightly as he began packing his single suitcase.

"Don't worry. Those kids will keep an eye on the Penetrator and that nigger cop who came along. We'll know their every movement within half an hour of it happening."

"In half an hour that son-of-a-bitch could kill us both."

"Not with that black cop in tow. You're the one who identified him as Nero. He's not going in for any illegal stuff. So don't sweat it." Lessor left to get whatever rental car he could locate this early in the morning, while behind him a nervous Joseph T. Armbrewster finished packing.

After more than fourteen hours flying time and only four hours sleep, Mark Hardin met Jim Nero in the coffee shop of their hotel. Neither of them felt as though they were functioning on all cylinders. Nero poured coffee for Mark from an insulated pitcher.

"My mouth feels like the Russian army dug latrines in it," he said by way of greeting. "When do we go to the police?"

"We don't." The Penetrator took a sip of the steaming brew.

"What do you mean we're not going to the locals for help?

"I don't work that way. Oh, I want them to come in and pick up the pieces after it's over with. That's just the icing on the cake. But I do my own dirty work. That is why I have the reputation I have and am as effective as I am."

Jim Nero shook his head. "I can't go along with that. What we'd be doing would be illegal."

"Look, I bought bringing you along, now you have to pay the price of throwing in on the deal."

"My way or the highway, eh?"

"You got it." Jim Nero sighed heavily, then brightened as the Penetrator went on. "We'll make a canvas of the hotels, but my guess is they went into the back country. They're probably out at one of Armbrewster's *fincas* or that commune Lessor ran."

"Then they're definitely headed this direction?" Lessor asked the grinning thirteen-year-old, who stood almost wriggling in anticipation of the reward he would receive.

"*Sí.* They hired a jeep and loaded in some luggage, then drove off. Armando and Manuel stole a car and followed. Whey they saw where the men went, they called. I was at the *telefón* nearest here."

"Thank you, my man." Lessor handed the boy a five-dollar bill. Then he turned to those gathered around him. "All right. We're going to be attacked in less than half an hour. Everyone take your positions. This time we get the bastard. I want the light machine gun crew to keep your eyes open. Watch every approach, including behind you. You've got to be able to cover the entire open area of the compound." He turned to Joseph Armbrewster, handing him a Ruger .44 Magnum. "Here. You know how to handle this Blackhawk, I've seen you use one before. Make sure every shot counts."

Armbrewster accepted the gun gratefully. As it stood, so far as they knew, only the Penetrator and that incompetent cop, Nero, had the whole story. Kill them and they would be free to go on with their plans. He tucked the long-barreled piece into his waistband. "You're doing a great job, Brad. Here's where it's all going to end. We get the Penetrator and we go on to win the whole ballgame."

The Penetrator pulled his rental jeep into the brush at a point he judged to be roughly a quarter mile from the commune. He and Jim Nero climbed out and Mark opened his arms case.

"You take this and two concussion grenades," the Penetrator instructed, handing Nero a Mac 10 Ingram. "You have your own sidearm. Here's three extra magazines for the Ingram."

Jim Nero had fired the Smith Model 76 and had been entirely unimpressed with the 9mm submachine gun, but he gained an immediate appreciation of the balance and comfortable feel of the silencer-equipped .45-caliber chopper the Penetrator had given him. He slipped the spare magazines into his waistband and pocketed the grenades. In his eyes the anticipatory light of battle had already begun to glow.

"I want you to come in on the back side, circle around so you're at a forty-five degree angle from me. I'll take 'em from here. That way we'll have enfiladed fire on them with the only avenue of exfiltration into the sea. The main thing is to see that Lessor and Armbrewster don't leave the area alive."

Nero frowned. "What if they surrender?"

"Take them if you can, but cover your ass first. I don't want to haul you out of here in a pine box."

Jim Nero smiled inwardly at the Penetrator's use of G.I. slang. With every passing hour he learned more about this strange, hard man with a consuming mission against crime. As an Air Force Reserve Captain, Jim had done a tour in Viet Nam as a liaison officer to the grunts, so he knew well the source of the Penetrator's expressions.

"Watch your own tail, buddy, and I'll keep hold of mine."

They parted, moving off quietly into the undergrowth. Mark moved soundlessly, one hand and arm working ceaselessly to fend off branches to prevent revealing noise. He spotted and avoided two pendulum traps and a Ho-Chi-Toe by the time he abruptly halted his forward movement.

The Penetrator's sensitive nostrils had detected the faint odor of tobacco smoke. For a moment he felt only contempt for the slackness of smoking discipline among the enemy, but then he quirked his lips into a grim grin, thankful for the advantage it gave him. Cautiously he started his advance.

Two minutes later he located the outpost. A single men lounged under a tree, taking frequent drinks from a clay jug of water and puffing on a cheap locally made cigar. After a few moments to determine that the man was definitely alone, Mark moved in closer. When the lookout rose to relieve himself, the Penetrator's strong arm snaked out, clasping a tough hand over the startled man's mouth, bending back his head while the keen-edged blade of his Enos sleeve knife bit into flesh in the triangle at the base of the neck, between the collarbones.

Slicing to both sides, the Penetrator's blade severed the carotid arteries and opened the larynx so that the thrashing guard developed a new mouth, out of which no sound came as he died. Blood gouted out, and the Penetrator stooped to wipe his hands, arms and knife clean before moving out. Another three minutes and he reached his jump-off point. Across the clearing to his left he saw a movement that indicated Jim Nero was in position.

As an armed man scurried through the open, the Penetrator raised his silenced Sidewinder and touched off a burst.

Chapter 17

HIGH-PRICED VICTORY

Down range, the Penetrator's bullets chewed up plumes of sandy soil and bit into the running man's legs. He screamed in pain and tumbled into the dust.

Damn! Should have fired from the shoulder at this distance, the Penetrator thought. A moment later he realized they were expected when a light machine gun opened up, spraying the foliage with slugs, some fifty feet from him but in the right direction. Have to silence that gun first, his combat-trained knowledge prompted. Cutting at a sharp angle to put some buildings between him and the automatic weapon, Mark charged the position.

Swinging wildly, the man behind the M-60 tried to traverse onto this suddenly appearing target before he reached cover. As the bullets stitched closer, the Penetrator saw Jim Nero rise from his concealed position and lob a concussion grenade that bounced once and disappeared behind the sandbag pit from which the machine gun chattered.

When the grenade went off, a great column of dust and debris rose into the air, along with ammo cans and bits of uniform and rock. Could have been better with a fragger, the Penetrator thought, but no cause to complain about results. He didn't falter in his direction, speeding past one hut and loosing a long burst through an open rear window. Rifle slugs spattered into the thatch near Mark's head and he dived into a forward roll.

Coming up, he unclipped a hand grenade and pulled the pin, tossing it lefthanded into the hut loaded with snipers. The M-27 went off with a crunching roar, starting the shack on fire. Men screamed and several, unarmed, ran from the building beating at flames on their clothing. Like Jim Nero, the Penetrator held his fire. All the while, Mark's eyes darted around the area, seeking some sight of Armbrewster or Lessor. More rounds zipped past his head, one tugging at his field jacket.

Looking to his right, the Penetrator located the source of this new fire at the same moment Jim Nero flipped his second concussion grenade in the window. The hut walls blew out, collapsing the roof, which burst into flames. Through the smoke, the Penetrator spotted a powerfully built man, with wide bands of silvery hair over his ears, rushing toward the distant beach. Armbrewster!

Mark jumped into the open, to be confronted by three more armed men. He swung up the Sidewinder and chopped one to his knees. The second took cool aim and began tightening his finger on the trigger when Mark's second burst caught him in the chest. He spun away, leaving a single man.

It took no mean genius to realize the score in this blitzing attack. The hastily recruited soldier raised his hands, crying aloud, "*¡Lo esto a merced de usted, señor!*"

Hell! After all his fine talk about taking prisoners,

what was he to do with this man proclaiming to be at his mercy? The Penetrator took two quick steps forward and delivered a hard left to the prisoner's jaw. As he did he catapulted violently forward and to the left.

As he turned, trying to recover balance, the Penetrator saw Brad Lessor standing in the doorway of a hut, spraddle-legged, a chattering, bucking MP-40 in his hands. With a start, Mark realized that only one person would have tried that hard to save his life. He added speed to his spin so that he faced the action in time to see the end results.

Jim Nero's shove propelled the Penetrator to safety, but his momentum carried himself into the line of fire. Six rounds from Lessor's SMG caught the black detective in the chest and gut, while three cut down the kneeling gunman, who was holding his head. Before the severely wounded policeman hit the ground, Mark raised his Sidewinder and ticked off two three-round bursts.

The first blast from the Sidewinder caught Lessor across the knees, the second splashed into his body low in the stomach. He dropped his weapon and crumpled to the ground in a bloody heap. Mark dashed to Jim Nero's side, kneeling and cradling the wounded cop's head in his arms.

"Jim . . . *awh*, Jim. Why didn't you stay out of this? I . . ."

Captain Nero wet dry lips and spoke in a fading whisper. "I wanted to be in on the kill. Funny . . . never figured it'd be me bought it."

A thick lump surged in the Penetrator's throat and his voice came in a croak. "Hang in there, Jim. We'll get you out. We'll send for an evac." Suddenly Mark Hardin was back in the stinking jungles of 'Nam, watching and fighting while his buddies died on all sides of him, somehow miraculously being saved himself from all but minor wounds. Unbidden and unnoticed, tears began to stream down his face.

"Won't make no difference," Jim Nero gasped. "I've had it but good this time. Get on with what you're doin'. You still got Armbrewster to bring in."

Mark ignored everything but the dying cop in his arms. Bending low he repeated over and over, "Hang in there, Jim. Just hang in there." After a couple of seconds, Jim Nero gave a convulsive heave of his muscular body, shuddered, and stopped breathing. The Penetrator began to rock on his heels, his voice taking on a melodic timber as he started chanting the Cheyenne warrior's song. At last he rose, mindful of his situation and the reality of what yet needed doing.

Raising reddened eyes to the sky, he called aloud, "*Hokkâ hē!* It's a good day to die!"

A moan from the doorway of the nearest hut stopped Mark as he strode from this scene of death. Incredibly, Lessor still lived. In four long strides, Mark reached his side.

"Help me. Oh, God, it hurts so much. Please help me."

Looking down on the wounded man, recalling the pain-twisted features of Captain Jim Nero as the black policeman was dying from Lessor's bullets, the Penetrator moved the muzzle of his Sidewinder until it centered between Lessor's eyes.

"No! Oh, *no*, please! I didn't mean anything," Lessor bleated, his voice quavering with terror.

"Kiss your ass good-bye, you bastard," the Penetrator said grimly as he tightened his finger, pulling the trigger on the Sidewinder all the way through to full auto.

Mopping up took only a matter of minutes. With the ragtag army dispersed, the Penetrator took a handy car to transport himself and Jim Nero's body back to the jeep. Only one problem yet remained.

Joseph T. Armbrewster was still on the loose.

Chapter 18

IT'S ALWAYS AN UNLOADED GUN

Joe Armbrewster had not run from the battle in fear, but had operated under a plan of his own devising. By now all the loose ends had been taken care of for him by the Penetrator. Who knew what might come of that? Perhaps the bastard himself would be blamed for what had happened.

The way he had it set up now, he'd finish off the Penetrator and have only his version of events to tell the law. Smiling grimly, he crouched low over the wheel of his idling Cadillac convertible, accompanied by four trusted bodyguards of long standing, waiting. When he heard the sound of an approaching vehicle, engine laboring mightily, he gauged it carefully, then hit the accelerator, dropping the transmission into low.

Armbrewster's heavy car leaped forward, crashing into the front fender of a fully laden farm truck. In his haste, Armbrewster had timed it wrong and missed the Penetrator. Keeping his foot to the floor, he cranked the wheel violently and ground free of torn metal, while the Puerto Rican driver of the damaged pickup shrieked imprecations in colorful Spanish, the likes of which had never been taught in the public schools. Fishtailing, Armbrewster roared off down the narrow road.

The Penetrator had to brake sharply to avoid rear-ending the stalled truck. Easing his way around he saw Armbrewsters' car in the distance. He fumbled to release the jeep's windshield and then raised his Sidewinder to snap off a short burst.

Two bullets smashed into the rear of Armbrewster's Caddy, puncturing the spare tire in the trunk, while three more smacked into one bodyguard who tried to return fire. Armbrewster gave the powerful engine more gas, suddenly having his role reversed to that of pursued instead of pursuer and, dust billowing behind him, was soon lost to Mark's view.

The Penetrator fought down the sudden burst of anger that momentarily clouded his mind. Grasping the wheel tightly, he sped after Joseph Armbrewster.

Winding up through a large grove of trees, their chase progressed onto the main highway leading back to San Juan. Despite the difference in relative power, Armbrewster's Cadillac held only a slim advantage over the jeep the Penetrator had rented from *Automoviles Gonsaga*, the Hertz of Puerto Rico. Twice Mark lost sight of Armbrewster, only to discover him again, some thousand yards ahead, racing steadily toward the city.

Mark hoped his adversary would avoid the slow-moving traffic and narrow streets of San Juan. If Armbrewster only realized it, there lay greater security for him and even greater danger for the Penetrator. If the police stopped Armbrewster, they would be confronted by a man of wealth, a local property owner, and person of influence. On the other hand, how long would they listen to a wild-eyed, blood-stained man with a submachine gun?

As they flashed down toward an intersection where a small green-and-white sign with an arrow pointing to the right advised, AEROPUERTO, Mark sighed with relief when Armbrewster's desire to escape overcame his logic. When the vehicle ahead of him slowed to turn off, Mark crowded his jeep to the limits to close the gap.

Once the range narrowed, the Penetrator stuck the silencer of his Sidewinder over the lowered windshield and fired another burst. Bullets starred the glass to Armbrewster's right, after passing through the chest of another bodyguard. Armbrewster panicked, turning hard left down another road that circled to the east, through the outer fringes of ramshackle *barrios* on the edge of San Juan, leading eventually to El Morro Castle, the oldest fortress in U.S. territory. Tires shrieking into the turn, Mark followed resolutely.

Twisting and turning around slower traffic, the fleeing man and his nemesis raced toward the distant, growing walls of the ancient fortification. Begun by the Spanish in 1539, El Morro guarded the entrance to San Juan Bay. In ensuing years, wars with pirates, the English, the French, and finally the Spanish-American War had all but demolished the old bastion. Recently a heritage-conscious people had successfully pressured for its restoration. Its five tiers of ramparts overlooked the luxury hotels of the Strand, and in some part helped mask the squalid desolation of the *barrios*. Toward the wretched sprawl of the latter the chase now led.

Crumbling buildings of stone and plastered mud flashed past as the Penetrator fought to get the utmost out of his laboring jeep. Chickens fluttered to perches among the limbs of bedraggled trees, and small children fled before the speeding cars. People shook their fists and cursed, as ahead of him, Mark saw a street vendor's cart smashed to ruin by Armbrewster's Caddy. Dust raised from the cobbled streets settled on wet wash hung on lines from the balconies of tenament-like dwellings. Housewives sighed in resignation to this accustomed depredation and set about redoing their labors, while the straining cars raced on toward the rear entrance to the old fort.

A low stone wall and high, iron-picket fence surrounded the tourist attraction, now temporarily closed for another phase of restoration. Armbrewster slewed through an open service gate and plunged down a ramp into the castle grounds. Gaining slowly, the Penetrator rushed after him.

Mark came upon Armbrewster's abandoned Cadillac, its nose rammed against a stone post, steam from its ruptured radiator shrouding it in damp fog. He braked to a stop. The Penetrator hastily hid his automatic weapon and started on foot toward a distant staircase leading into the fortifications where he'd seen Armbrewster and his henchmen disappear.

As the Penetrator reached the last stone step, where the way before him opened up onto an artillery battery revetment, a shadowy figure leaped at him. Mark dropped below the charge, the man's body sailing over his head. He came up to deliver two forceful *shuto* chops to his attacker's kidneys. Staggered by the blows, hurting but not out of the fight, the man spun to renew his attack.

Mark shot out a stiff right arm. His aim perfect, the Penetrator felt bone give beneath the heel of his hand. The man fell to the ground, his jaw sagging at an odd angle, blood spurting from his mouth. Mark hurried to a low parapet, searching for the fleeing pair that remained.

On the next revetment down, Mark spotted

Armbrewster and his bodyguard, hurrying toward a ramp that would take them closer to the seething waters of the Atlantic far below. Mark ran to one of the many gradual inclines, which allowed for the movement of cannon, and descended quickly. As he rounded a projecting wall, stone chips sprayed his cheek, cutting deeply, and a moment later he heard the sound of the shot. Ducking back, the Penetrator drew his Star PD.

Taking a cautious peek around the corner, Mark spotted his foe. Kneeling behind a large bronze cannon, Armbrewster and his remaining bodyguard took steady aim at the point where the Penetrator had disappeared. Two flashes and slight puffs of smoke heralded the enemy's bullets in time for Mark to get out of the way. The Penetrator came into the open again, firing and starting a weaving course as he charged the guns before him. Blood trickled from his cut cheek and sweat stung his eyes, but his aim was true enough to keep down the heads of those who opposed him.

As the Penetrator neared their place of concealment, Armbrewster disappeared over the parapet. His bodyguard rose to face the oncoming threat. He fired a pair of hastily aimed rounds, then steadied. His increased stability did him little good, though, as the fourth bullet fired by the Penetrator struck him just below the diaphragm, gusting the wind out of him and driving him backward, so that he fell to the flagged flooring unconscious long before death claimed him. Taking time for only a brief, reassuring glance, the Penetrator hurried on, seeking Armbrewster.

Mark found his way impeded by carriage-mounted cannon and other implements of sixteenth century warfare. Armbrewster had led him into the completely restored portion of the old fort. Tantalizingly close, Armbrewster's powerful shoulders showed briefly before he ducked behind another bronze demi-culvern. The Penetrator used this advantage to close the gap. In a matter of seconds he found himself close enough to hear the rasping of Armbrewster's breath.

"Give it up, Armbrewster," he called. "You haven't got a chance."

"The hell I don't! Barr's a raging maniac. You didn't know I'd found that out, did you? Between us we've eliminated all the other witnesses. So who will they believe? Me or the infamous Penetrator?" His voice changed, grew high-pitched and tinged with an edge of madness.

"I've got the formula, you know. Nothing or nobody can stop me from using it! First I'll purify this country, then all the Western Hemisphere and Europe. At last the greatest feat of all, I'll rid Africa of its curse."

"You're as crazy as Barr, Armbrewster. Where can you go? Who'll hide you, aid you? Not even the Ku Klux Klan would back this insane scheme. There's evidence enough to prove your involvement. With your money you could hire a good enough attorney to see you'd be out in a couple of years, if you went to jail at all. Put down your gun and take your chances with the law."

As the Penetrator spoke he wormed his way between the massive tubes of two iron-bound, bronze cannon, inching closer to the frenzied man who defied him. When he reached a good position Mark made ready to jump his adversary. At the same instant, Armbrewster surged to his feet.

"I'll never be taken," the demented millionaire cried. "There's only you who knows and you'll die right here!"

Mark crashed into the bulky form of Joe Armbrewster, staggering the man, but not carrying him off his feet. Armbrewster swung one powerful arm like a club, knocking Mark free of his hold. As the Penetrator sprawled backward, Armbrewster advanced, fists balled, striking telling blows on Mark's chest and face. Struggling against a fuzzy haze of unconsciousness, the Penetrator tried to position himself so he could take back the initiative. As he set his heel, his ankle turned painfully under him. He stumbled and tripped over an anchor chain that secured the carriage of 32-pounder cannon. In the next instant, he pitched backward over the ancient artillery piece.

Instead of pressing his advantage to end it then, Armbrewster chose once again to seek flight. He pounded down the ramp, at the head of which the Penetrator still lay in tumbled confusion. As Mark started to his feet, Armbrewster, glancing behind him, halted and whirled, drawing the .44 Magnum given him by Brad Lessor. He fired twice rapidly as the Penetrator charged him.

Both bullets missed and Mark came on. Armbrewster squeezed again. Behind the Penetrator a jingling sound announced the parting of one link of the chain that secured the huge cannon. An ominous rumble followed the clatter of the severed strand. Looking behind him, the Penetrator saw the carriage begin to move down the ramp. It gained momentum as Armbrewster fired a fourth time. The gun carriage came to a sudden halt, snubbed up tight by the chain on the opposite side. The Penetrator threw himself face first to the stone flooring.

From below him Mark heard Armbrewster's terrified scream as the retaining bands broke on the carriage and the heavy tube catapulted off its trunion and cartwheeled through the air. With a slow *whup*ing sound like a lazy propeller, it revolved over the Penetrator's prostrate form. Then, as if in slow motion, it descended, smashing its thousand-plus pounds of weight down onto Joseph T. Armbrewster, who feebly raised his arms as though to ward off this harbinger of doom.

When the resounding noise of the falling tube had faded away, the Penetrator rose and walked to where he could look down on the red smear that had been Joe Armbrewster.

"Well," he observed with a shrug as he turned away, "as they say, it's always an unloaded gun that accidentally kills someone."

EPILOGUE

'Tis better that a man's own works, than that another man's words should praise him.

—L'Estrange, *On Being Judged*

Tendrils of steam rose about the glistening, naked bronze form that squatted by a low fire in the center of the sweat lodge. Pungent odors assailed Mark Hardin's nostrils as he inhaled the thin streams of smoke coming from the teepee of twigs that maintained the heat of glowing stones from which the steam rose. Outside, a skin-covered tomtom throbbed, and, as though he had reached a decision, Mark moved.

Raising both arms above him, palms open in supplication, he threw back his head. The cords of his neck bulged, the blood vessels seeming to pulse in time with the rhythm of the drum, while his throat worked convulsively as he began a singsong chant.

"Hear, Oh Great Spirit, Mightiest of Fathers, this prayer of a warrior of the People," he wailed in Cheyenne. "Send my words to that High Place, the eternal hunting ground, to the ears of mine enemies, slain in battle. Let their High Spirit know how heavy is my heart at the taking of life. Send down the Spirits of the East and of the West to bring the light of wisdom so that my footsteps do not falter, though my head be bowed, my shoulders fallen, and my heart most heavy. Send down the Wind Spirits of the South and the North to blow clean my High Self, purging me of the blood guilt of those whom I have killed so that others might live."

On and on the prayer went for two hours, each phrase carefully repeated, lest the entire ritual have to be begun again from the first. At the end of this time, the Penetrator picked up a braided horse quirt, its strands knotted around small, sharp shells, and lightly lashed his back, symbolically mutilating himself in mourning for the death of Captain James Nero. Undeservedly Mark had carried with him a burden of guilt for the black policeman's death that could be as deadly to him as the unpurged blood guilt of those he'd killed to bring an end to Armbrewster's mad scheme. Now he let out that grief in tears and lamentations, remembering aloud the good qualities of the black detective who had given his life to protect Mark's own.

This completed, he drank out of a horn spoon a red-black brew taken from a hanging skin pouch. He continued to consume the vile-tasting mixture until it forced its way back out of his body. Then Mark fell onto a pine bough bed in an exhausted sleep.

Twelve hours later he awakened, refreshed and

feeling whole in spirit as well as body. Leaving the sweat lodge he dived into the depths of a shimmering pool of black water that had filled the lower levels of the old borax mine where Willard Haskins had built his Stronghold. Mark swam briskly, without pause, for half an hour, then climbed, dripping, from the pool and dried himself with a rough, nubby towel.

He slipped into a pair of cutoffs and moccasins, and climbed the stairs to the level above where he took the elevator to the "tower" room. For the first time since his ritual purification he spoke, calling aloud the names of his mentors. Only silence answered him.

On the bar he found a note explaining that David Red Eagle had gone to Saugus, to the experimental farm there, to purchase a young buffalo. The note's author, Willard Haskins, had gone into Barstow to pick up groceries and the mail. Mark was encouraged in the missive to build himself a stout drink and relax over a basketball game on TV. Compliant to suggestions of that sort and completely at peace, Mark built himself one of the stoutest of drinks, a Singapore Sling.

As he added the final dash of club soda to the tall glass, his mind digested the meaning of the professor's note. A dinner of roast buffalo hump meant a new mission coming soon. His mouth watered at the savory memory of the delicious, rich meat. He had just finished the longest and most convoluted case in his violent history, and he regretted the implication of once more exposing himself to the chance of meeting that inevitable bullet, knife, or bomb that would end his career, but curiosity overcame his desire for release.

Sipping idly at his drink, Mark walked into the Operations room, checking the big display board there that laid out potential crisis spots and current missions under consideration. From a pocket under a yellow Condition Two numeral, he took a Manila folder. He walked back into the tower room and turned on the television, tuning in the "NBA Game of the Week." Mark seated himself in a leather-covered recliner and opened the file.

The Celtics took second place to the pages inside, as the Penetrator began to devote more and more of his attention to a report of rumors of discord among Air Force personnel on several bases inside the U.S. The whole affair puzzled Mark. In a time of peace, uneasy though it might be, when the game of Harass the Military had been all but forgotten by the ambitious and unscrupulous politicians, the professional agitators, peace creeps, and zealous leftists, what could possibly be causing this?

The promise of a buffalo feast, he felt sure, might soon result in his learning the answer.

THE PENETRATOR'S COMBAT CATALOG

This is the seventh volume of the Penetrator's Combat Catalog. As developments continue to occur in the fields of weapons, equipment and vehicles, they will be tested, evaluated, and the best will be incorporated into use by Mark Hardin. Those found best suited to the Penetrator's use will appear in the pages of this continuing catalog. As mentioned before, testing takes time, so we will not be able to include a volume of the catalog in each episode of the Penetrator's adventures, but they will be inserted as often as the need arises.

In previous installments, we have cautioned readers regarding local, state and federal laws governing the private ownership of automatic weapons, destructive devices, and explosives. Some of the equipment used by the Penetrator is available for retail distribution, but many are one-of-a-kind developed especially for Mark Hardin. Thirty-three out of fifty states allow ownership of automatic weapons and suppressors. Some of these, however, restrict destructive devices (mortars, recoilless rifles, etc.), so we urge you to make a careful check of all regulations before attempting to purchase items you see in these pages.

Lionel Derrick

THE ROLLINS SYSTEM

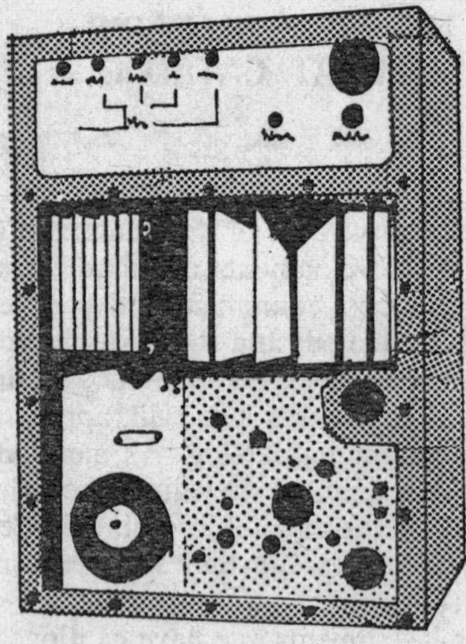

This electronic home surveillance and security system features: a master control that monitors the environment on a 24-hour basis; hand-held remote control unit for turning on interior and external lights; a choice of instantaneous or delayed alarm modes; wireless installation; fire detectors; an emergency power source; beep tone to monitor entrances and exits; an electronic light switch for turning on interior lights during a forced entry; an outside alarm siren and an automatic dialing and recorder message of illegal entry or fire that can be made to any outside telephone.

The system is manufactured by Rollins, Inc., with offices in 44 States, the District of Columbia, and Mexico. Cost of installation depends on the extent of the area to be covered. Basic unit has a suggested retail price (without installation) of $465.

Performance

Since the Rollins System operates off of sound waves picked up by its remote detectors, and has its own self-contained power source, it is virtually foolproof. The master control can be set to activate the system from a varying scale of sound intensity. In operation the system proves as excellent as the company claims.

HIKER'S HATCHET

Mark Hardin's Hiker's Hatchet combines three tools in one. It is a hand axe, a knife, and a saw. Through the hatchet head, from inside the handle the double-edged saw blade-knife extends 8 inches. The hatchet head is made of three 1/8'' sheets of 440C stainless steel.

This handy tool was designed for S&S Arms owner, Sid McQueen, by Joseph G. Cordova, 1450 Lillie Drive, Bosque

Farms, New Mexico. It sells at a suggested retail price of $150.

Specifications

Axe Head: Cutting edge, 4''; Thickness, 3/8''; Length, 5½'';
Saw: Length, 8''; Thickness, 1/4'';
Knife: 8'' x 1/2'' x 1/4''
Weight: 3 lbs. overall
Overall Length: 15''
Composition: 440C stainless steel, axe head laminated 1/8'' plate.

Performance

The Hiker's Hatchet holds up to the most rugged conditions. It cuts through manzanita and mesquite with the ease of a chain saw and all sharp surfaces hold an excellent edge. Like all new products, the machining of the handle could use some attention, but the various components extend themselves for operation with little effort and the locks hold.

THE GLADIATOR

The Gladiator quarter-sword is another exclusive design of gifted knifemaker Joe Cordova. Made of 440C stainless, it has a gladiolus-shaped blade similar in design to the Roman short-sword, hence the name. It is double-edged and hollow ground. The Gladiator comes with an unusual scabbard, the Reversa-sheath, designed by Sid McQueen of S&S Arms. The Gladiator can be obtained from Joseph G. Cordova Knives, 1450 Lillie Drive, Bosque Farms, New Mexico, and is priced at $225.

Specifications

Blade: Length, 8''*; Width, 1-3/4''
Thickness: 1/4''; Guard: 3-3/4''
Overall Length: 12-1/2''

Weight: 10 oz.
Weight with sheath: 1 lb. 4 oz.
Handles: Black linen micarta
*Blade length is measured from tip to center of quill.

Performance

The Gladiator carries well; balance feels comfortable in the hand. Four-forty C is probably the most common steel used today by custom knifemakers and is known for the excellent edge it keeps, given proper care. Small saplings, bamboo, and other tall grasses yield to the Gladiator as easily as with a machete. It is not an "everyman's" knife, like a Randall Made or K-BAR, but for the afficionado, it makes an excellent addition to collections or survival gear.

PRODUCT UPDATE

CORRECTION: In No. 28 Penetrator: THE SKYHIGH BETRAYERS, on page 182, a Winchester Model 11 field grade shotgun was incorrectly illustrated as being the Mossberg M500 ATP 8S. For an accurate example of the Mossberg, get a copy of No. 25 Penetrator: FLOATING DEATH, where the ATP 8S is excellently illustrated on the cover by artist, George Wilson.

On Page 176, Ava is shown without

the CO_2 cylinder and its retaining bands, directly below the barrel.

PRICE CHANGE: The Detonics .45 ACP Pistol, illustrated in No. 27 Penetrator: ANIMAL GAME, now has a factory suggested price of $435 for the blue steel model, $475 for the nickel finish. A little checking by Lionel Derrick indicates that the Detonics can be obtained from discount stores, such as ALCO and K-Mart for as low as $345.

NEW MODEL: The first 100-unit production run of the SS-IV Sidewinder SMG reached the market in August, 1979. It features a 3-stage progressive trigger for SF, 3 RB & FA.

THE SPARTAN "C" PRESS

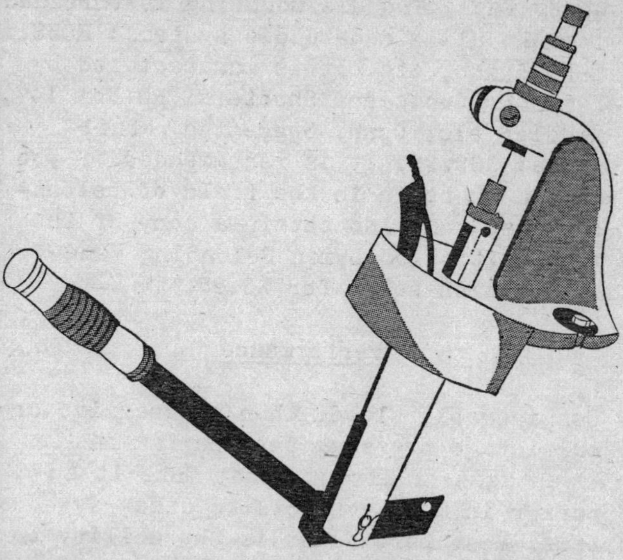

Lyman's Spartan "C" Press provides the Penetrator with a low cost means of loading critical ammunition for rifle and pistol. It is a single stage press, meaning that each operation is done one step at a time. Depriming, sizing, and priming are done with a single die as one operation, then the loading is performed on an unattached powder measure (as opposed to a multistage press where the powder measure is an integral part of the press) and the casings then returned to the press for bullet seating and crimping (where needed) on another die. The Lyman press is of cast metal with a sturdy steel ram that has a universal shell holder machined into its upper face. The die mounting is threaded to take all standard die systems: RCBS, C-H, Lyman, etc. It is manufactured by Lyman Products for Shooters, PO Box 147, Middlefield, Conn. Suggested retail price: $69.95. It is recommended if you intend to begin in the field of reloading that you also obtain a copy of the 45th Edition of Lyman Reloading Handbook, which sells for $6.95.

Performance

Considerably slower than progressive or multistage presses, the Spartan has advantages of its own that make it superior in many respects to other systems. Most particular is the ability to produce uniform, dependable loads of match quality.

THE ATCHESSON CONVERTER

On those rare occasions when Mark Hardin must use an M-16 or the AR-15 semi-auto version, he prefers to modify it with an Atchesson Converter. This allows the firing of .22 long rifle ammunition. The benefits derived from this are threefold: an increase in accuracy, a slight increase in cyclic rate of fire (in full-auto mode), and the obvious one of lighter ammunition to carry around. The three-piece unit (for M-16) and one-piece converter model (for AR-15) are both manufactured by Tom Atchesson and distributed by Numrich Arms Corporation, West Hurley, N.Y. 12491. Suggested retail price for the Model 1 (M-16) is $99.95. The unit comes in a high-impact poly-vinyl case along with one 30-round magazine.

Performance

The Atchesson device is inserted into the receiver of an M-16 or AR-15, replacing the bolt assembly. The tapered chamber insert at the front end and rimfire firing pin allow for use of .22 long rifle rim-fire cartridges. Although highly criticized in an article in American Rifleman for powder fouling in the AR-15 model, when using Federal Cartridge Co. Hi-Power ammunition in the M-16 version such fouling is not present. In fact at a recent law enforcement seminar the Penetrator's converter fired over 2,000 rounds through an M-16 at full-auto with only one failure to feed, resulting from leading in the converter chamber. Less than a minute was needed to run a wire brush through the converter and reinstall it in the piece. Powder fouling appears to be a function of ammunition quality with Federal being far superior to other makes.

The cyclic rate of fire increased to

nearly 1,000 rpm, with a noticeable improvement in accuracy. Part of the cause for the latter comes from the greater inherent stability of the 40-gr. .22 long rifle bullet over the needlenosed, semi-boat tail 50-gr. .223 ball round used by the military and police. In an AR-15, the Model 2 semi-auto version functions satisfactorily, but neither converter work well in a CAR-15.

With a pair of spare magazines loaded and extra ammunition along, a back packer can easily carry a thousand rounds without noticing the increase in weight in his pack—using the Atchesson Converter turns the somewhat useless M-16 into a formidable weapon.

GAS PENCIL

Mark Hardin used a CIA Gas Pencil in No. 3: CAPITAL HELL, while modifications and improvement were being made to Ava. Originally designed for use by the OSS in WWII, this small pocket weapon could handle three different loadings. The first was a .38 Special cartridge with a ball round; the second, a capsule of prussic acid (cyanide) for assassinations; and the third, tear gas. The design was later reworked for the CIA and used by various intelligence agencies until recent times. From 1946 until 1969, when the Gun Control Act of 1968 went into effect, the manufacturer produced a civilian model, the MK 3, that fired tear gas only. Because it was in .38 caliber, it had to be discontinued under the restrictions of the GCA '68. CAUTION: If any reader comes across one of these, do not try to use a .38 ball ammo cartridge in them. The chamber unit of the MK 3 is made of cast aluminum and will not withstand chamber pressures of a bullet-fitted cartridge. All three models, MK 1, 2, & 3, are not available for sale at this time, with the possible exception of getting one from a collector.

Specifications

Caliber: .38 Special. Length: 4 1/2''. Base diameter: 9/16". Weight: 3 oz. Action: Single shot, spring-driven firing pin. Construction: MK 1 & 2, all steel, MK 3 has aluminum chamber. Ammunition: .38 Special Ball or Shot Shell; .38 CN cartridge (Red seal); CN-DM cartridge (Yellow seal); Prussic acid (Pale Blue seal).

Performance

The chamber and barrel unit screw into position in the body of the pencil, ahead of the recoil plate. The recoil plate is center drilled to allow the spring-driven center-fire firing pin to extend far enough to strike the primer. When loaded, the pencil is carried with the firing mechanism in the safety position, an inletted slot in the side of the barrel-shaped receiver. To fire, the small knob is drawn out of the slot and pulled rearward with the thumb, then released. The gas pencil is purely defensive in nature, except when used with cyanide. The reason is simple: Who wants the torn fingers and circular puncture in the palm of the hand from firing a .38 Special bullet cartridge with some 3.5 grains of powder?

When using the pencil with a prussic acid charge, it is necessary to take an antidote injection some two hours prior to use and breathe deeply of an amyl-nitrate ampule immediately after discharge. Under test conditions, the range with a ball round was extremely limited, accurate bullet placement being nearly impossible beyond a five-foot distance. To be truly effective with tear gas, it was almost necessary to stuff the muzzle up the assailant's nose. Needless to say, when using <u>any</u> gas cartridge, it is wise to be on the <u>upwind side</u> of your target.